Meeting at last...

    I started to leave but a little click told me there was someone at home after all. I turned around and met Ed McKinney head on!

    Oddly, there was no hint of surprise. He looked me over and then something akin to a smile brought a twist to his face.

    "You must be Rachel. I hardly recognized you. You're certainly not a teenager anymore."

    His voice was low but very precise and clear which somehow conflicted with the strange expression on his face. He looked so ordinary! Then, I realized that I had been expecting something akin to, as Mrs. Campbell had put it, the devil incarnate. At that moment the memory of the little bottle of pills hidden in the cabinet reminded me that he was anything but ordinary, no matter his appearance.

Other works by Annis Ward Jackson available on Kindle:

Blue Ridge Parkway Plunge: Rachel Myers Murder Mysteries
Christmas Tree Wars: Rachel Myers Murder Mysteries
The New River Blues: Rachel Myers Murder Mysteries
Appalachian Trail Mix: Rachel Myers Murder Mysteries
Mountain Mourning: Rachel Myers Murder Mysteries
High Country Coverup: Rachel Myers Murder Mysteries
Mahogany Rock Falls: Rachel Myers Murder Mysteries
Brown Mountain Breakdown: Rachel Myers Murder Mysteries
Highland Games: Rachel Myers Murder Mysteries

Jingle Bells, Shotgun Shells: Ellis Crawford Murder Mysteries
Bought and Died For: Ellis Crawford Murder Mysteries
Exit Here For Murder: Ellis Crawford Murder Mysteries

Into The Deep: A Story of Resolution
Into the Twilight: The True Origins of Abe Lincoln
Patchwork: Short Stories and Essays of the Appalachian Mountains
Christmas Trio: The Night the Lights Went Out In Christmasville; The Light in the Window; The Last Christmas Doll

Nonfiction:
Practical Gardening: Sensible Solutions for Down-to-Earth Gardeners
Ophelia's Satirical Diadem: Herbs in Shakespeare's HAMLET

Blind Malice

First in the Rachel Myers
Murder Mystery
Series by

Annis Ward Jackson

Blind Malice:

A Rachel Myers Murder Mystery

Copyright 2009 by Annis Ward Jackson

This novel is a work of fiction. Names, characters, places, and incidents are either used fictitiously or are the product of the author's imagination. Any resemblance to any actual persons, living or dead, locales or events are purely coincidental.

Acknowledgments

I owe my gratitude to many people along the way, my mother who fostered my interest in words and reading, many excellent teachers, especially Dr. F. David Sanders who was director of the honors program and my adviser at East Carolina University.

I am especially grateful to my husband whose support has been essential and absolute in all my writing ventures.

Chapter One

Since the nineteen sixties, when the first ski resort was built in the Appalachian Mountains of North Carolina, many of the highest and stateliest peaks have fallen beneath the sword of that most beguiling conqueror, the tourist industry.

It was on one of these ski slopes, at the time only a harsh slash of empty brown down the side of Moseley Knob, that I fastened my gaze and held on tightly, seeking to block from my consciousness the scene around me. My efforts failed.

A small knot of mourners stood under the tent, opposite me across the open grave. A loose corner of the tent flapped gently but steadily in the slow breeze. Fallen leaves skipped over the newly turned soil, gold and red competing with the lavender mums and pastel carnations that banked one end of the grave. Bits of mica in the soil gleamed in the autumn sun, giving the scene an almost incongruously carefree appearance.

I sighed in relief when the sound of the preacher's voice ceased. He handed me a shovel and as I scooped up a small portion of the soil the smell of freshly turned earth rose to my face. I turned the shovel sideways and a hollow death rattle carried up from the grave as tiny stones struck and rolled off the metal exterior of the casket.

My mouth was bitter and the slight breeze seemed to grow colder. Inwardly, I shuddered but was able to keep my disquiet from showing except for a slight stumble when I returned the shovel to the preacher's waiting hand.

As I looked up, the sun cast a pink glow on the tombstones and turned the flowers a garish hue before it moved behind a cloud. I tried to keep my eyes away from the tombstone at the head of the newly dug grave. I could not.

Mary Wilson Myers, 1939-1982, Beloved Wife and Mother graced the right side of the granite stone. On the other was Paul E. Myers, 1936-. The new information would soon be added.

Turning quickly aside, I made my way down the narrow footpath, drawing away from reaching hands that sought to comfort me. My father was gone; what need was comfort? It would not bring him back.

He had died as he had lived, alone and blind. Blind because glaucoma had taken his sight, alone because I, his only child, had chosen to live over two thousand miles away in Flagstaff, Arizona, and caught up in my own little world, had not been to visit him in nearly two years.

Lying there against the pale gray satin, dressed in his best suit, he had looked so young and at peace. His white hair was fresh and combed just as he had always worn it. His eyes were closed naturally and gave no indication of the blindness that had undoubtedly helped to bring him to his death.

I recalled only too vividly the expression on his face the last time I had seen him. He begged me to move back home or at least somewhere closer. His anger and disappointment was clear but he tried hard to stay in control.

His voice nearly broke when he said, "Flagstaff's over two thousand miles away! Isn't there some job here, or near here, Charlotte, Raleigh, somewhere?"

I also recalled my reaction to that. "Dad, you don't understand. I love my job and Flagstaff is where it happens to be. I love these mountains as much as you do but I can't make a living here.

"What would I do, take a job at Sheppard General, making barely above minimum wage? Dad, I didn't go to college for four years to get my nursing degree to do that."

He interrupted me, "Rachel, I don't recall a single time that I've tried to run your life. But, what about here, this farm? It's our life, all our lives, you, your mother, me, Isaac!"

"But, Dad, it could never be my whole life! Mom's gone, you're blind and in ill health. And look at Isaac. He's nearly eighty years old!. I tell you what, Dad. Sell the farm! Yes, sell it and come to Flagstaff and live with me. We could…."

Again he interrupted, but his voice had gone quiet. "You're crazy, Rachel! How could you even suggest… how could I possibly leave here? My life is here, everything. Leave here blind and sick and go somewhere foreign to sit by a window where I wouldn't know what I was looking at even if I could see it?"

His voice changed, became even quieter and cold.

"If you don't place any more value than that on what I've worked for all my life, to hell with you! You're not who I thought you were!"

Stubbornness swelled within me, would not allow me to run to him, to hug him and apologize. Tears stung my eyes and my throat tightened.

"All right, Dad. If that's the way you feel…"

We said goodbye the next morning with an unnatural formality. Isaac and Dad's housekeeper, Mrs.

Campbell had watched us, hope on their faces that we would resolve our differences before we parted. Their hopes were not met.

A hand laid gently on my shoulder tore me from my thoughts. My self-control vanished.

"Isaac, oh, Isaac, he's really gone!"

I yielded to grief, stifled until this moment and leaned against him. He patted my shoulder awkwardly.

"It's all right, Rachel, it's all right. He didn't suffer none. Doc Hartley said his heart gave away so fast he never felt any pain."

I bit my lip, took a deep breath and began to dig in my purse for a tissue. Isaac was quicker and offered me his neatly folded handkerchief. I wiped my eyes and blew my nose with easiness possible only around someone as familiar as the old man.

"You just better be glad he never laid there and suffered like your mama done!"

I stared at him, searching his face for the cause of the tightness in his voice.

"Isaac, you know I'm glad he didn't suffer. What's wrong with you? You've been short with me ever since I arrived yesterday!"

His eyes narrowed and the weathered skin tightened around his mouth.

"Well, there's something wrong, all right. But, this ain't no place to be telling you. I'll come by the house this evening and we'll have a go round at it."

Isaac's face softened, relaxed, and his own grief showed plainly. He reached out and touched my shoulder, then moved stiffly away, old friend of my youth. My youth? No, of my life.

When I was just a baby, Isaac Starling had come to my father, nearly destitute and still in the throes of depression over the drowning death of his wife and son many years before. Paul Myers, then a young man, just beginning his life as a husband and father, saw in Isaac a value far above that apparent to anyone else. They were distant cousins but I always believed that Isaac subconsciously assumed the role of surrogate parent.

My father was an only child and a change of life baby, his father 45, his mother 42 when he was born. She died in 1954 but his father lived for another eighteen years. I remembered my grandfather vaguely as a tall white-haired man who dandled me on his knee and recited a long rhyming poem about an old gray goose.

So, Dad found in Isaac a partner, a willing listener, a quiet peaceful man who acted rather than spoke. My father was fascinated with gadgets and was always trying out some new contraption on the farm machinery. Isaac stood by him patiently and did his utmost to assist him while others in the small mountain community of Laurel Hill smiled and shook their heads.

If a new gadget failed to work, Isaac accepted it, and without a word returned to the old one. If it succeeded, he would offer one of his rare smiles and shake my father's hand.

Although the years separating them were only ten, Isaac carried an ancient look in his blue eyes as if he had already lived one lifetime and this second one was very quiet compared to the first. He became a fixture on the place and lived in a converted apple house near the orchard. Few people in the community could remember when Isaac Starling had not been there working by my father's side.

While the sounds of dirt against casket carried down the hillside, I watched as Isaac climbed into his battered old Dodge pickup. It was the same vehicle in which he had taught me to drive nearly twenty years before. It ground to a start and then gravel crunched under his tires as he drove away.

The few distant relatives who had turned up for the funeral approached me again. A woman with a haggard expression and wispy gray hair spoke first.

"I don't reckon you remember me. I'm Gracie, your papa's second cousin on his daddy's side. I saw you a few times when you was a youngun'. I used to worry about you being an only child."

She sniffed and wiped her nose with a pink tissue.

"I'm awful sorry about Paul's passing. There ain't many of us Myers's left in these mountains."

As if she had exhausted her entire supply of words, she stepped aside. Each of the small group voiced similar sentiments. Then, one woman, younger than the rest and appearing vaguely familiar to me, stepped forward.

"I'm your daddy's cousin's wife. Well, second wife, really. He was a widower when I married him and now I'm a widow."

She expressed the same sympathy as the rest of the group about my father, hesitated and then continued. Somewhere between words of comfort for me and praise for my father, an aggrieved tone had crept into her voice.

"I reckon Paul had a rough enough time to wear out anybody's heart. And, it appears he wasn't about to get help from anyone!"

She stared accusingly at me while I tried to make sense of her words.

"Else he could have told them people to leave off pestering him about selling his land. I know a man finds it hard, asking his kin for help. But to ask and be turned down, well, that's a painful matter. Looks to me like…"

The Reverend Clayton Jones, his funeral suit flapping in the breeze, interrupted the woman, apologized, and then turned to me.

"Rachel, you come on around to our house for supper tonight. No reason for you to be there at home by yourself."

I acknowledged his invitation and murmured answers to several other people who had waited to speak to me. As quickly as possible, trying not to offend any of them, I turned back toward the women but they were gone. An old minivan was easing out of the church driveway onto the road. With a thin stream of blue smoke from the exhaust, it wheezed out of sight.

"What in the world?"

I remembered my father telling me about someone making him an offer on his property at one time but that had been four or five years ago. And what did she mean about someone asking his kin for help and being turned down?

Before I could dwell on the odd suggestion, several stragglers filed by with solemn words about my father.

"Knowed him since he was a young boy. He made a good man."

"Lent me money and sent Isaac over to do my chores when I broke my leg that time."

"Went out of his way for anybody that needed help."

Wade Gwynn, my father's friend and attorney, was the last to approach me. Holding both my hands, he tried to speak without tears. I could see his grief was much deeper than what showed on the surface.

"I'm sorry I wasn't much help to him there toward the end. But, since Ed McKinney began to spend so much time over there, I felt like an intruder. Paul really changed, Rachel. He became so distant and suspicious that he wouldn't allow anyone except Ed to help him in any way."

"But, Wade, I don't understand. What did Ed McKinney do for Dad? I thought he worked for the bank. He wasn't around the last time I was home."

Wade ran his hand across his sparse hair in obvious exasperation. "He does work for the bank, as a loan officer. But that obviously didn't take up all his time. I guess you haven't heard that he was the one that got rid of Mrs. Campbell nearly three months ago. Well, not directly, I suppose. Just made it so uncomfortable for her that she wouldn't go back any more. She took a job with some summer people and she's in Florida now.

"Ed threatened Isaac too but that didn't work out too well. Isaac threatened him right back and told him he'd go and personally bring you back from Flagstaff if he tried to keep him away from Paul."

"What..." I began, but Wade kissed my cheek quickly and stepped back.

"Honey, I have an appointment in a few minutes that I must keep. But, you come by the office on Monday, all right? We do need to talk."

Wade's hastily spoken words certainly cleared up my curiosity about Mrs. Campbell. I had noticed on first entering the house that it was not as clean and neat as usual. It hadn't seemed logical that she would have stopped coming so soon after Dad's death.

I felt myself slowly but surely sinking into uncertainty as the questions mounted up. First, why had my father kept the seriousness of his heart condition a secret from me? What was the source of Isaac's strange behavior and Wade's hint of something wrong with my father's financial affairs?

And, Cousin so and so's scantily veiled suggestion that I had somehow refused to help my father was almost bizarre!

Suddenly I was exhausted. The lengthy flight from Flagstaff yesterday, only two hours of sleep last night, and the funeral not over yet, at least not until I left the cemetery. I turned and took my last look at the grave. The flowers had paled in the evening light. As I walked away I could still hear the dull sound of the dirt being shoveled into the grave.

The distance to the house was not far but was slow and tedious. It had been years since I had driven very much on these mountain roads. Dad or Isaac had always been available on my visits to drive me wherever I wanted to go. And those places had been few. Home for me had always been just the farm, Dad and Isaac. And, where did all this traffic come from? I could remember driving this far without meeting a single vehicle.

The rental car was stiff and hard to control on the sharp curves. I thought of Dad's old Oldsmobile and how it would hug the curves and plow right through snow and mud. He sold it only when his vision made its final plunge into complete blindness.

After graduating from high school, Dad had tried different jobs over several years and had finally joined the Navy intending to make it a career. He had twelve years of service and was only thirty-two when a boiler exploded on a ship where he was based in Norfolk, Virginia. He had no other serious injuries but his eyes were permanently damaged.

The navy gave him a medical discharge and he came back to Laurel Hill. His vision stabilized and stayed that way until he reached the age when his eyes began to change naturally. By the time he was sixty he was totally blind. From then on he depended on Isaac and Mrs. Campbell for everything.

I wheeled the car onto the long driveway that wound toward the house. Yellow maples whirred by like flashes of light. Blackgums made burgundy streaks in the timber and even the oaks by the pond had belied their usual brown and turned a coppery red.

I had always loved the way the house was not visible from the main road. Then, suddenly, around a sharp curve, there it stood. Nothing extraordinary, just a simple two-story farmhouse with a one level kitchen added on the south side, and a barn and outbuildings.

The tires sang over the smooth asphalt and it was only then that I remembered my astonishment the day before when I arrived and realized that the driveway had been paved! It was about a half mile long and must have cost a small fortune. That Dad would spend that much on… well, another question for Isaac.

I sat in the car, chin propped on the steering wheel, and stared at the house. I didn't remember it being so small. Barker, Dad's collie, greeted me as I left the car. I stooped to pat his head and he swung his tail gratefully. He was old, at least for a collie. Dad had bought him the year after I left home so that made him about thirteen. I remembered it so well because I had teased Dad about how it felt to be replaced with a dog. He had laughed and patted me on the head.

I wandered about the yard, unwilling to face the cold emptiness of the house. Barker trotted beside me, pausing when I did. Bright yellow Chrysanthemums, still called "October Roses" by many mountain folk, purple Ageratum, and a few Shasta Daisies grew in small clumps against the brick underpinnings of the house.

In what had once been a vegetable garden, asparagus ferns had turned to gold and rhubarb leaves lay flattened by frost. In the back yard a large bunch of Hollyhocks grew by the old well. Their burgundy blossoms were long gone, replaced by rows and rows of brown seedpods that rattled in the eternal mountain breeze.

These were all that remained of my mother's flower gardens. I turned away from the noise, so like the hollow sound that had just minutes before struck so cruelly at my heart. I broke off a few of the mums to take inside.

My mother had always loved to garden and my most vivid memories of her were those that concerned her flowers in some way. Actually, it was difficult to separate the two.

There had been in her a deep-rooted love for the soil. She was content so long as she was able to work in her flower gardens without interruption. Her hands in the soil seemed to serve as a therapy of sorts. No problem was too difficult to solve, no pain too great to bear if she could spend time amidst her flowers. She divided them, replanted them, weeded them, loosened the soil around some, and firmed it around others.

Mountain winters were torture. Long and sometimes harsh, they were occasionally disastrous to her precious gardens. A familiar sight was Mother by the kitchen window looking out upon her snow-blanketed garden, her expression so evident of the concern she felt.

Dad would come in and watch her for a moment, then chide her gently, "They'll still be right there when spring gets here, Mary."

Mother would nod briskly and go back to her chores but the lilt in her voice and the quickness in her step would not appear until spring when the snow melted and the first green shoots burst through the ground. There was sheer worship in her eyes, a reverence anciently instilled, for the small lavender Crocus that flagrantly displayed it's color among the dead stems of last year's perennials.

I had inherited my mother's love of growing things but not her casual cottage gardening style. In back of my small Spanish style house in Flagstaff, the space was neatly and precisely divided into herbs, perennials, and Hostas.

Just outside my kitchen door was a small raised bed where I grew tomatoes, peppers and eggplant. David had often teased me about my penchant for order and I had many times countered by declaring that the entire world would do well to consider a good dose of my order.

Many plants that would not survive the dry heat of summer in southern Arizona thrived in the cool temperatures of Flagstaff. I loved brightly blooming perennials and tasty fresh herbs and vegetables, but most of all I adored my Hostas. I had been an enthusiast for many years and had accumulated a collection of the most unique specimens available.

Suddenly I shivered. The sun had eased down almost to the crest of the mountain and was casting streaks of fiery red over the white clapboards of the house. I rose wearily from my seat on the steps and turned to go in.

"Rachel?"

Isaac had removed his funeral clothes and now wore his usual faded flannel shirt and carpenter jeans. He moved slowly and I was reminded again of his age and how long he had been here on the farm with my family, working, existing. He had never accepted much in return except a small salary and a place to live.

I unlocked the door with the old-fashioned skeleton key that held a small round tag from the First Colony Bank. Isaac followed me inside. My Pullman case, still unpacked, sat at the foot of the stairs.

I headed for the kitchen not allowing my eyes to linger on any one object that would remind me of Dad. I settled the few mums into a vase and set them in the window over the sink. Two nearly ripe tomatoes lay on the windowsill. I bit my lip against tears that threatened to rise again.

The teakettle was heavy with the morning's water so I emptied and refilled it. The pilot light made a plopping noise and then settled down to wrap the kettle in pure blue flames. Isaac sat on one of the heavy stools that my father had made during the first year he owned his sawmill.

I plunged right in.

"Isaac, Dad's cousin, I've forgotten his name, the one who lived here in Laurel Hill when I was a little girl, well, his widow said something to me at the funeral today that really has me puzzled. I've tried to figure it out but I just can't. I…"

Isaac kept his eyes on the teakettle as he spoke.

"That was Johnny Myers's widow. Johnny passed on a few years ago and she kind of clung to his side of the family. Don't pay her any mind. She always did have her nose where it didn't belong."

"But, Isaac, this was something about someone trying to force Dad to sell his land and him asking his kin for help and being turned down. Since I'm the only close kin he had left, I assumed she was talking about me but I don't have a clue what she was getting at!"

My voice had risen to near shrillness and Isaac's face darkened. He shook his head slowly, not the response I had hoped for.

"Well, Missy, if it's got that far I might as well tell you right now and be done with it."

He settled back and looked me squarely in the eye. Never before had I seen such an unconcealed expression of anger in his face.

"Youngun', your dad was taken terrible advantage of for a long time and nobody around here could do a damned thing about it!"

I swallowed hard, could hardly believe my ears. Short of dad-gum or dang or blast, I could never recall having heard him curse before. The words finally sank in and I asked, "But, Isaac, how… who…?

He brought his hand down over his face, smoothing his wrinkled skin, temporarily giving himself a younger look. As soon as he removed his hand, he looked older and more tired than before.

"I hate to be hard on you, Rachel, but if you could have been here a little more often, you might could have stopped it. I know you and Paul had words but... well, anyway, you see, Ed McKinney got to coming around here, first time was just a few months after your last visit. He'd always come on Lydia Campbell's days off and always when I was busy.

"Took me a while to figure out that he was up to something. He's lived here in Laurel Hill and worked for the bank for nearly twenty years and never showed any interest in making friends with your dad before. Don't reckon he even paid his respects when your mama died.

"Well, anyway, I snuck around a little and all I could find out was that he was supposed to be an agent for some corporation that was buying up land around here. It wasn't long before Paul stopped talking to me at all about what was going on here at the farm.

"Matter of fact, he told me more than once not to bother with keeping anything up around here, that there was no reason to. He lost interest in the apple orchard and finally sold all the cattle and the sawmill. McKinney took care of the sale."

I was astonished. "You mean...? I didn't know he'd sold the sawmill! He never wrote a single word about it, not even a hint!"

"I'm not surprised at that," Isaac went on. "It got to the point that the only person who knew anything about your dad's business was Ed McKinney. But, that wasn't what I started out to tell you.

"That woman back yonder at the funeral, what she was talking about was, Ed McKinney has told folks around here that your dad had serious money troubles and when he finally got low enough to ask you for help, you turned him down!"

I was dumbfounded. Confusion stormed in my brain as I tried to sort out what I had just heard. Dad in financial trouble? No way! Never once had he let on to me that he needed money. Quite the opposite, his letters all sounded as if everything was going very well.

"Isaac, I don't understand. Dad never once asked me for help. And, why should he? Even without the sawmill, he always had the cattle, the apple orchard, the tobacco allotment, and I know he had a reasonably good savings, plus his Social Secuity and Navy Pension."

"Rachel, I told you. He just seemed to give up on everything. All he'd talk to me about was the old days when we were young and your ma was alive. And he couldn't understand how his finances had got so bad. Most of all, he couldn't understand how you could turn down his asking for help.

"Now, I couldn't believe that you had, Rachel, and I tried to convince him of that. He wouldn't listen. Said you'd just completely grown away from him living so far away out there in Arizona State. I knew there was something crooked going on but I couldn't convince him of that either."

We sat silently for a few moments and then Isaac continued.

"You see, McKinney read Paul's mail to him, even got to where he picked it up at the Post Office like I used to do. And he wrote his letters for him, too. Lydia Campbell used to do that but McKinney took over everything. Why, there at the end, he near just about moved in with Paul. Same as fired Lydia Campbell and dared me to come around!"

"But, Isaac, why didn't you let me know? You could have written or called or something!"

"Well, when Lydia left I figured that was the last straw so I snuck around the house trying to find something with your address or telephone number on it. Couldn't find a thing. Your mama's old roll top desk had been cleared completely out. I asked your dad and all he knew was Flagstaff.

"Anyway, I even tried to ask McKinney and he told me point-blank that if I needed to get a message to you, he'd be glad to include it in Paul's next letter.

"Why, the only way Old Doc Hartley knew how to get in touch with you when Paul died was to force the information from McKinney by telling him he'd get the sheriff's department involved if he didn't cooperate."

"But," I protested, "there must have been some way you could have gotten in touch with me. You know more than anyone how close Dad and I always were."

Isaac's voice lowered and he spoke slowly.

"You sure about that, Rachel? Two years is a long time to go without seeing someone you're so close to."

I could not bring myself to admit to Isaac that my reasons for not coming home for nearly two years had very little to do with the quarrel with Dad. The first summer David and I took a vacation train trip through several national parks.

The next summer, two nurses had contracted a very contagious virus so I had to fill in for them when we couldn't get temporary help. Then I had a bad case of flu myself and was out of commission for a while. And it had been almost too easy to rationalize.

After all, Isaac and Mrs. Campbell would look after Dad. He didn't need financial help.

Flying after nine-eleven was such a hassle.

I knew none of these were really valid excuses. The truth was that I had been coasting along, complacent and easy in my life with David and didn't want to interrupt it with a trip to North Carolina.

This was the first time I had allowed David into my thoughts since I arrived in Charlotte on Wednesday morning. He had driven me to the airport in Flagstaff with a casual air, trying to stay away from the subject that had caused the recent weeks of tension between us. Before I walked to the boarding gate, he reached for my hand.

"Rachel, I know it's selfish of me to ask you at a time like this, but... I know you won't have much time, with the funeral and all, but think about us some, at least. I'll accept whatever decision you make.

"But, remember what I really want is you as a wife, not as a live-in lover. Everything is going so well with the company, all it would take to make my life complete is for you to say yes. I know that's considered old-fashioned today but that's the way I feel."

I pulled away, not answering, just giving him a quick peck on the cheek. I hurried into the loading tunnel without looking back. As the plane taxied down the runway, I stared back at the terminal. As the plane rose higher and higher the building grew smaller and smaller until it was only a dark rectangle on the misty expanse of the tarmac.

On the long flight from Flagstaff, he had occupied my thoughts between bouts of confusion about my father and a growing sense of dread that I tried to push away.

Isaac was saying, "...and like I said, two years is a long time to go without seeing somebody in your pa's condition."

I forced the last strains of David's face from my mind.

"But, Dad never indicated to me that there was anything very serious wrong with his heart. I knew he had mild angina and that it was under control. I'd gone more than a year before without a visit. I wrote and I called frequently.

The dead silence that followed was more revealing than if the old man had shouted.

"You're thinking that this time was a lot different than before, aren't you? Isaac, how was I supposed to know about Ed McKinney? And I did call Dad, I don't remember how many times. Christmas, his birthday in February, Easter and always on Father's Day. He never gave me even a hint of anything being wrong."

Almost before the words were out of my mouth, I remembered. The last call, Father's Day in June, Dad had sounded strained, unnatural for someone who liked to talk as much as he did.

Suddenly, a sequence of times began to take place in my mind. Unremarkable until I began to reflect on them, I recalled a gradual change in Dad's letters also. Sometimes he used words that I'd never heard him use.

Occasionally I had wondered if Mrs. Campbell had been absorbed with something else when Dad was dictating his letters. She always pounded them out on the old manual Remington that Dad had used forever to type his farm records on.

The type certainly had not changed. The letters continued right up to the last one, with his old-fashioned signature across the bottom. As I concentrated, ignoring Isaac almost completely, something else came to me.

"I knew it, something was different! Even though they were typed, Mrs. Campbell's letters were sort of uneven, a little on the sloppy side. She was always running off the page because the right margin wouldn't hold. And the spelling and grammar were always inconsistent because she tried to write them exactly as Dad spoke."

The more I contemplated the matter, the clearer I could see them. I couldn't remember when the letters had changed but they definitely had. I raised my eyes to Isaac. It was clear that he did not share my enthusiasm for the value of my discovery. He stroked his chin thoughtfully as if giving me time to offer something more.

"So, all that tells you is that Ed McKinney began to write Paul's letters at some point. We already knew that!"

"No, Isaac, that's not what I mean!" I could hardly contain myself. "See, that's where the letters began to sound so unlike Dad. Stiff and formal, almost like he was dictating a business letter."

Isaac frowned, then, "But what does all that prove except what we already know?"

"It proves, Isaac, that Ed McKinney changed the way Dad said things to the way he'd say them."

"But I still don't see…"

"Isaac, if Ed McKinney wrote things differently from the way Dad told him to, he could just as well have written things Dad didn't tell him and, more to the point, left out things Dad wanted to say, or ask!

If he left out Dad's appeal for financial help from me, which he certainly did, how was Dad to know? Then when he received my next letter and I never mentioned anything about it, Dad just thought I was intentionally ignoring it."

My stomach lurched suddenly and for the first time since I arrived in Laurel Hill, the situation hit me full force.

"My God, Isaac, he died thinking I didn't care enough to help him!"

A sizzling, steaming interruption, the teakettle boiling over. We busied ourselves for several minutes soaking up the water around the gas burner. Silently Isaac rung out the towels and spread them on the counter edge. I poured the water into an old familiar brown teapot. Then I slowly stirred my too-hot cup of tea.

"The real question is, Isaac, what could Ed McKinney possibly hope to gain by changing Dad's letters like that?"

Chapter Two

Afternoon sun streamed through half opened blinds forming bars of light that seemed to imprison me in bed. Through bleary eyes I half-recognized the colors and shapes on the tied back curtains. Very sophisticated ballerinas on a white background. I had chosen that fabric myself in the eleventh grade.

My room had not been redecorated after I left home. There was my high school graduation group picture, my yearbooks on the nightstand and my favorite photo of Dad and Mom on the dresser.

The photo brought back in a sickening rush the telephone call, the funeral arrangements, the funeral itself. My chin began to quiver and I thought what a relief it would be to break down and cry here all alone, to give in to it all. Then I remembered Dad's exact words after Mom's funeral.

"Honey, you know your mother wouldn't want you to go on grieving. If she were here right now, what would she say to you?"

I had sniffed back my tears and answered, "She'd say, 'Rachel, finish your chores and then you'll have time to do something you really want to do'"

Still good advice. I slid out of bed and headed for the bathroom, turning up the ancient thermostat in the hall just enough to knock off the autumn chill.

I had to stoop my five foot ten frame a bit to see my face in the mirror while I brushed the tangles from my hair. As dark auburn as ever but with a few streaks of gray beginning to show. That was hereditary. Dad had been completely gray by the time he was forty-five. My eyes were hazel, again like Dad's, but right now they were streaked with red from my long sleep. I went back to the bedroom and pulled on jeans and a heavy sweater.

The hall clock said one thirty p.m. That didn't surprise me. I had barely pulled up the covers before exhaustion completely overcame me. By the time I got to the kitchen the outline of what was left of the day was beginning to take shape. I would stay in and rest up for what would be the next leg of the ordeal on Monday – all the legal workings that followed the death of anyone who owned any property at all. I shoved all that behind me for the moment and put on the coffee.

The refrigerator was well stocked. While the bacon sizzled, I thought back over the conversation I had had with Isaac the night before concerning the letters from my father.

After a few minutes consideration I brought out my laptop and sent an e-mail to a colleague of mine in Flagstaff. Sandy and I kept a key to each other's desks at work and she could easily find the letters from my father and mail them to me. I was not sure if they would yield any evidence concerning Ed McKinney's motive for not writing my father's request for help.

But at least I could prove to Isaac or anyone else concerned that nowhere in that entire stack of two years worth of letters was there any such appeal.

Suddenly aware of the implications of that possibility, I realized that there were two sides to the question, or answer as it were. I must find my letters to Dad. With both sets…suddenly it became very important to me that Isaac and Wade Gwynn or anyone else know that there had been some confusion, that I had not refused to help my father.

Indeed, I had often reminded him that my investment of what he and I jokingly referred to as my inheritance from my Grandmother Myers, thirty-five thousand dollars from the sale of an obscure piece of property in another county, had been very wisely invested by David and had doubled itself several times over.

In fact, that was the only link with David that I had allowed to become solid and tangible. His brokerage firm handled my investments and he was very conscientious about reinvesting anytime he was sure to add to my "fortune."

Once he had teasingly said, "You know, I could just make an unintentional mistake and lose all your money and then you'd have to marry me!"

I knew there was no danger of that happening. David was almost painfully honest, both in his professional and in his personal life. Maybe that honesty was part of what fed the reluctance I felt about marrying him, or just marriage in general. He had told me in detail about his previous marriage. And was honest enough to lay the blame where he thought it belonged, on himself.

"I was young, immature, right out of college, but even that was no excuse. I just refused to see anything anyone else's way. Debra was a few years older than I, just enough to make her attractive to me, then enough to cause a problem later on. I tried to make her what I wanted her to be. She had been a career woman since long before she met me. I tried to do away with that pretty soon after we were married. I wanted a stay-at-home wife. You know, the apron and slippers at the door bit. I have to say that she was game enough to try it for a while but it didn't work out. That's why we split up."

I had given him a raised eyebrow That's what I meant kind of look and he answered quickly, "That's all over, Rachel. I understand now. I'm a lot older and I hope, a good bit wiser. Don't you see that I'd never expect that of you?"

My first marriage was enough in itself to make me extremely cautious about a second one. Grady and I married just out of college where we had met as juniors. He was lovable, fun, sweet and totally irresponsible. His whole approach was, If I'm sorry and I say it, everything should be forgiven.

Money problems, extramarital affairs, denials, and then apologies: that was our entire eighteen months of marriage. We separated and our divorce was final one year later. I went back to my maiden name and began to look for a job somewhere far away. That was how I landed in Flagstaff, Arizona..

Enough apprehension lingered that even now, over a year later, David and I were no closer to the altar than when he first proposed. But, as I had promised him, I would definitely spend some time thinking about us while I was here in Laurel Hill.

The kitchen door rattled open, startling me until I realized that Isaac had a key. He was a bit more relaxed after a night's rest and a few of the worry lines had faded from his face.

"I thought I bought some stuff for sandwiches," he said, eyeing my bacon and egg plate.

"Oh, this isn't lunch, Isaac. Would you believe I've only just gotten out of bed?"

"Well, I guess so," he grunted, "considering yesterday. But it's still beyond me how anybody can sleep after sunrise, anytime."

I finished eating under Isaac's watchful eyes. Then I reached over to the counter and opened my laptop in front of me. There were no e-mails but then I hadn't really expected any. I had suggested to David that we didn't need to correspond every day, that this should be a sort of time-out while I made up my mind about our future. Isaac leaned over to look at the screen.

"Now, why do you need something like that," he questioned. "Surely you can still use a telephone!"

"Oh yes," I answered. "Let me show you my cell phone." I showed him how it took photographs and played music and several other functions that made him shake his head. His response was less than enthusiastic.

"Well, if it doesn't work any better than most of them I've seen, it sure won't be any good around here. Not much use having something that you have to climb on top of a mountain to use. I reckon the whole world has gone nuts for this technology stuff.

"What gets me is, way back there, when these computers were just getting started, the big benefit was going to be how much faster everything could be done.

Well, before they had a computerized cash register, I could go into Miller's Store and get what I wanted and whoever was there could add it up with a pencil and paper, hand me the ticket and take my money just like that.

"Now they have to punch in a long string of numbers or run an item over a scanner a dozen times before it'll pick it up. Don't seem much faster to me."

"Yes, Isaac," I said. "But that's not all a computer does. Keeping records is a big part of it, also. Think about how little space it takes to keep hundreds of files on a single DVD as opposed to the amount of paper that much information would cover. And the security, too. That's always a big factor. Paper files can so easily be destroyed or copied…"

Isaac interrupted me. "Now, right there is where I've got you. Last year what they call a hacker got into the computers at the savings and loan and copied everybody's records. They didn't even know it had happened for several days.

"Now, if crooks had broke down the door to get into the building, there's no way they would have had time to copy all that stuff in one night. And they sure couldn't have carried off that much paper without somebody seeing them."

"But, Isaac, there's more to it than that. Take my rental car. It has a GPS on it, a Global Positioning System. It works off several satellites. If that car was stolen or just wasn't turned in on time, they could pinpoint where it was within a few feet. And ships and planes have them and even some hikers carry them. Now, you have to admit that that is worth something!"

Still doubtful, he said, "Well, maybe."

I decided it was time to change the subject.

"Where would you say Dad kept his correspondence, letters from me, things like that?"

"Are you still fretting about that?" he questioned.

Suddenly his face went serious.

"Are you still thinking there's something important to be found in them letters? Because there ain't no wondering where they are. I saw them the morning before Paul died. I had misplaced my key to the tool shed and needed to get in there for a pair of tin shears. I knew there had been an extra key laying up on that china cabinet in the dining room for a long time. Things just always accumulated up there.

"Anyway, there wasn't no key, just Paul's bottle of heart pills that he kept sitting there because they were easy to get to when he needed them. I leaned the cabinet forward a bit to see if the key might have fallen down behind. Never found that key. But what I did find was a bundle of your letters stuck behind there."

He stepped into the dining room and returned quickly.

"See, here they are."

With hands both eager and trembling I rolled off the rubber band that held them together. The one on top was postmarked only a month before, the last I had written. The envelope felt thick, not surprising since I usually wrote several pages. I always tried to put in enough detail about my work so he could understand just what it was all about. I took the letter from the envelope under Isaac's watchful eye. A gasp slipped from my mouth and it was moments before I could speak.

"Isaac, there's not a damned word in here! They're just blank sheets of paper!"

The old man must have been just as flabbergasted as I because he did not reprimand me for my profanity. Instead, a bewildered look settled on his face. We stared at each other long and hard.

I believe at that moment we both realized that Ed McKinney was responsible and that the reason was something dreadful. He had destroyed my letters and replaced them with blank sheets. My father might have questioned their physical absence so McKinney could not very well toss them out. In his blindness, my father never knew the difference.

McKinney's purpose had been served. No one could ever read the letters and find out that McKinney was lying when he said that I had refused to help my father.

"That does it, Isaac! I want to talk to Ed McKinney right now! I want this explained!"

My hands shook as I looked for McKinney's number and dialed. An answer machine took the call. The voice had a faint thickness about it and was obviously not a typical mountain accent.

"This is Ed McKinney. Please leave your name and number after the tone and I will return your call." Be-e-ep.

I did not leave a message. I wanted to see him face to face. Meantime, Wade Gwynn should be able to give me more information toward clearing up this mess. I could not see him before Monday morning so I would just have to fill in the time with other things.

Isaac ambled off down the path to his little house saying to let him know if he could do anything for me.

And, with a wink, that I needn't think he hadn't noticed me cussin' like a sailor.

After a quick kitchen cleanup, I put on a hooded sweatshirt and sneakers to take a tour around the farm. I had paid only scant attention to anything since I arrived except the funeral arrangements.

Now I began to see what Isaac had meant about Dad letting the place go. Behind the house, at the back of the yard, a large grove of ancient oak trees grew in a wide arc. They had been limbed up for many years and had provided a shady area for a picnic table and chairs. The furniture, now covered with mildew and fallen leaves, was barely visible. Large dead limbs lay in piles and Poison Ivy wound its way to the tops of some of the trees.

Beyond the oaks, the nearest level strip of land on which the large burley tobacco allotment had always been grown lay empty except for a heavy crop of Goldenrod and Ironweed.

The apple orchard, once a source of great pride to Dad, was really in a mess. The trees, mostly heirloom varieties like Wolf River, Roman Beauty, and Henry had grown out of all proportion from lack of pruning. Long straight water sprouts grew from the crotch of limbs. A fungus of some sort that manifested itself in large hunks of black crud had invaded the orchard. The few pear and cherry trees were full of the nasty disease. Grass and weeds grew tall throughout the orchard.

Looking down to a field that once served as pasture for cattle, I could see impressions of drainage ditches, so newly dug that patches of fresh dirt still showed. The ditches stretched all the way to the paved road but stopped there. I could see scum covered mud where the water had stood after a heavy rain.

"What is the point in ditches that don't carry the water away from the field?"

Another something to discuss with Isaac.

A large new metal outbuilding stood at the back of the older wooden barn. I didn't remember it being there when I was last home. It was empty and obviously had never been used. The topics for discussion were mounting.

I closed my eyes and leaned against a section of old-fashioned rail fence that separated the barn lot from the apple orchard.

Everything was beginning to crowd in on me. The funeral, the letters, Ed McKinney, the condition of the farm.

I stood quietly, letting the cool mountain breeze gently waft over my face. As if to circumvent the coolness, something blew warm air against the back of my neck.

I whirled to find Dad's old walking horse gently snorting, nibbling softly with his big lips. I scrambled over the fence and threw my arms around his neck.

"Stayman, I had completely forgotten you, you old devil! Look how fat you are! You're beautiful!"

His name had come from his love of apples. As a colt he would reach over the fence and pull apples off the Stayman tree that was closest to the rail. Dad had ridden him until his impaired vision made it too risky.

I had learned to ride on Stayman but never let myself forget that he was Dad's horse. I had shared his love of riding before I left home for college and still rode when the opportunity arose in Flagstaff, although riding in a city park was nothing like riding the carefree wood trails here on the farm.

'Hey, you know, that's not a bad idea," I whispered to Stayman as I patted his round stomach. "That is if the cinch will still go around you!"

As if insulted he whirled and took off at a gallop, white mane and tail whipping against his coppery coat. Remembering the time I had worn sneakers on a short trail ride and ended up with blisters on the inside of both ankles, I went back to the house and found a pair of well worn boots deep in my bedroom closet.

Dad's very plain western saddle sat in readiness on the saddle tree in the tack room of the old barn and the bridle hung on a wooden peg above. Under its cover the saddle was dust free and smelled of neatsfoot oil. Isaac must have kept it cleaned although I knew Dad hadn't used it in many years.

At that image, I blinked back tears and hurried outside to whistle for Stayman. He twitched a bit when I laid the saddle pad on his back but stood patiently while I adjusted girth and stirrups. As soon as the bit slid through his teeth, he pawed the ground as if to say "It's been a long time, let's go!"

I led him away from the barn and mounted. It took a few moments to adjust myself to the saddle. Muscles in my thighs stretched painfully, reminding me that a while had passed since I had ridden. We started off at a brisk walk and I could sense that although he was full of energy, Stayman would not be difficult to handle. We met Isaac walking up the path, hands crossed behind his back.

"You take it easy with him," he cautioned. "Only time he gets rode is three, four times a year when Ben

Wallace picks him up for his wife to trail ride up in Virginia. It'd kill him to get him too hot in this cool air."

"Come on, Isaac, you know I'll be careful!"

A sharp pain in my calf muscle caused me to further remind him that Stayman would likely weather the ride better than I would.

"Well," he reiterated gruffly, "be careful of the both of you, then."

But, when I turned before entering the woods, he was watching us and waved as if to give us his blessing after all.

Chapter Three

David had once called me a romantic, a nature fanatic. While in the middle of a tennis game with him, I had suddenly ignored a perfect return and ran to the cyclone fence to inspect an unusual vine with miniature lavender flowers that sparkled like gems in the morning dew.

"Rachel, you don't just run off the court to look at a pretty flower. It could have waited!"

"I'm sorry, David," I said. "Just look, look how delicate it is. Growing and thriving here among all these weeds and dead things. And there, see, the whole plant is growing out of a crack in the pavement! Can you imagine that?"

David softened.

"It's like you, Rachel. Comes from an unlikely place and covers a lot of ground with its beauty."

I always became cautious when David began to talk romantic nonsense like that because I sensed the subject of marriage would follow. I would guide the conversation elsewhere, just like I was now guiding Stayman on the path I wanted him to take through the woods. Inside the cavern of white pine the colors became deeper.

Unfaded by sunlight, Virginia Creeper wound its way up a dead tree in a garnet swirl. On the ground wine red patches of Galax lay in splashes upon last years faded leaves. Jack, of Jack-in-the-Pulpit, had turned to a tight cluster of red berries that would fall to produce another crop of Jacks next spring. Emerald log moss that sparkled even in the shade carpeted a fallen tree like a green shroud.

A small red squirrel known locally as a Boomer chattered above me and somewhere I heard a grouse take off, flaying the air with its wings, the sound both startling and natural in the quiet woodland.

I kept going until I topped out on Rocky Face, the highest point on the property at about four thousand seven hundred feet. Great stretches of stone that covered the ground looked as though it had once been liquid and had run, forming great swirls in which white flint rock had been caught.

Vegetation was sparse, just a few pines that looked like overgrown Bonsai, all their limbs pointing in the same direction from the constant wind. Beeches were shrubs instead of trees, and a few patches of low-bush huckleberries had turned to crimson.

Far away I could see a curve of the New River as it wound its way north out of sight into Virginia. My friends and I had floated down that river on rubber rafts, paddled its smooth deepness in canoes, and shot its lesser rapids on inner tubes.

Dad and I had fished during the season and had spent hours in the spring and fall watching migratory fowl stopping off on their way north or south. It was a good feeling to know that the river would remain as it had been for future generations.

In 1974, Dad's friend and attorney, Wade Gwynn, had worked diligently to help mobilize people in North Carolina to protest a hydroelectric dam project planned by the state of Virginia. Had the project succeeded, I would now be looking at mountain coves back-washed with garbage.

Instead, before me lay one of the oldest waterways on earth following its natural path, unimpeded until emptying itself into the Ohio River. Although too young at the time to be very interested in the subject, I recalled very well my father and others in the community celebrating when North Carolina politicians from both parties formed an unlikely alliance and prevailed on President Ford to designate the New River as a wild and scenic waterway. That action effectively curtailed the desecration of a true national treasure.

Directly ahead of me, across a low ridge, was the property line Isaac had mentioned that bordered the Blue Ridge Parkway. The gray asphalt ribbon wove its way back and forth along the crest of the mountain, finally vanishing around a distant outcropping of rock.

As with the rest of the farm, I had forgotten how the woodland stretched in all directions. Up and over smaller mountains and down into hollows that began narrow near the mountaintop, then widened to almost cavernous depressions around the base.

It was in one of these places that, as a boy, my father had found where a Confederate soldier had camped and maybe died. There was still charred wood from the campfire when he raked back a deep layer of rotted leaves. He never found any bones, just a few buttons and the rusty barrel of a rifle. There were no battles that far north in the North Carolina Mountains but deserters would have found Rocky Face a perfect place to hide out from the home guards.

Most of the property that stretched out ahead of me was timberland and here and there the outline of an old log road showed through the thinning fall leaves. Dad had not cut any timber in this section for nearly twenty years but the roads remained with only a few scrubby bushes growing in the median.

Log roads made good horse trails so I chose one and walked Stayman around the mountainside. Halfway down the other side, back in a swag, I caught a glimpse of a shiny object near a thick, snarled grove of Rhododendron. Mountain folk called them Laurel Hells because it was nearly impossible to get through them. In fact, it was said by many older people, Isaac included, that Laurel Hill was simply a sanitized version of the massive Laurel Hell that the first settlers encountered when they arrived in our mountain valley.

Curious, I dismounted and tied Stayman to a sapling so I could investigate. Coolness struck me as I entered the dark tent of evergreens. Before my eyes could adjust I had identified the place by the sound of trickling water. It was the spring that Dad had always boasted of, swearing that it contained the purest and best tasting water in the world. A small ray of sun had penetrated the thick canopy and shone directly on a pint Mason jar turned upside down on a limb that had been cut off just for that purpose.

A spout made from a hollowed out half-log channeled the water from where it welled up from underground. The water fell off the end of the trough creating a small stream that followed the lowest level of the swag and then disappeared into the ground. A fat black spring lizard wiggled himself out of sight under a rock. I could almost hear Dad's voice, "When you see a spring lizard, it means the water is clean. They can't live in bad water."

I rinsed the pale green film from the jar, filled it and drank long and deep. The water was almost icy, and delicious.

Stayman snorted softly as if to remind me of his presence. I scooped out a small depression and waited for it to fill. After pushing back a few low limbs, I brought him to it and he drank slowly, as if for pure pleasure instead of from thirst.

I decided to walk a while. When I paused to allow Stayman a nibble of wood grass, I noticed a generous patch of wintergreen. Each tiny clump of fragrant leaves contained a cluster of bright red berries. My mouth watered in anticipation. I held the reins with one hand and bent down to pick with the other.

My memory served me correctly. In the nineteen fifties, a popular chewing gum manufacturer had tried to copy the flavor, even calling their product by it's colloquial name, Teaberry. But to one who had known the true flavor, the gum was a bland copy.

As I chewed on the berries I looked around the woods. So much to see if one knew where to look. The rectangular holes made by Pileated woodpeckers in a giant dead and rotting oak. A squirrel's nest in a live oak and beneath, patches of bare ground where wild turkeys had scratched for acorns and grubs. Just slightly off the trail, a young maple, perhaps five inches in diameter, heralded the beginning of rutting season, its bark scraped and frayed by the antlers of an amorous buck.

I would never have noticed the marker if not for the orange plastic ribbon. The wooden stake was driven loosely into the ground in the middle of a patch of an evergreen ground cover called Princess Pine. The garish ribbon was threaded through a small hole in the stake and tied securely.

It seemed to be a marker of some sort but I knew it was not a property corner post because they are nearly always metal and are driven deeply into the ground as permanent fixtures.

That was the end of my sightseeing. I went on to find over fifty of those same markers at various intervals down the rest of the mountainside. They were spaced about a hundred feet apart and were not in a straight line but wove back and forth until they reached a wide area at the foot of the mountain that contained about twenty acres of gently sloping cleared land.

My brain burned with curiosity but I could make nothing of it. I took a different way back home, over another ridge and down another steep log road but never saw any more of the markers.

Back at the barn I gave Stayman a good rubdown and turned him out into the pasture. He pawed a few times, and then dropped down to roll in an effort to loosen the damp hair on his back.

I tried to remember where Dad had kept his deeds and surveyor's plot of his four hundred and fifty acres of land. I finally found it in an old metal box in the back of his bedroom closet. I pored over the map, tracing my path up the log road, over the mountaintop and by the spring.

It was difficult to pinpoint the exact place where I had found the first marker. But from there on it became easier. I made X's with a red pen about where I remembered each marker's location to be. Soon a pattern began to develop. The markers were not by any means in a straight line. They zigged and zagged down the mountainside, dipping into the swags and then swooping out and down until they came to rest on the sloping area.

Try as I might, I could make no sense of the shape. Perhaps Dad had been planning to sell some land, but the markers were placed in too haphazard a pattern. No one bought land with such crooked boundaries.

Later, Isaac came by and I questioned him about who he might have seen going into the woods.

"Far as I know, only a few squirrel hunters. But, you never can tell. There's ways of getting into that area besides coming by the house here."

I left it at that, determined I was not going to spend the evening and all day Sunday wondering about it. I would take the map with me to Wade Gwynn's office on Monday morning and see what he made of it. Perhaps there was some simple explanation, but given the events so far, I doubted it.

Isaac accepted my invitation to stay and eat dinner with me. We didn't mention Dad, just talked about my ride on Stayman, and Isaac expressed an interest in my work. I found myself speaking proudly about my job as director of a chain of nursing facilities in Flagstaff.

I had started work as supervisor of nursing at the largest of the seven nursing homes. The job paid well and I advanced quickly. My co-workers swore it was because I was from North Carolina and thought work was holy.

The new position placed me mostly out of personal contact with patients. In my case, that was just fine. Many people I had worked with had the capacity for staying objective as they went about their work. My emotions clouded situations too easily. My heart could never accept some decisions that my head knew were necessary. So I was better off at my desk making decisions about where money was to be spent.

That was how I had met David. His firm handled some of the finances for the company. I didn't mention him to Isaac. I did not want to think of David tonight anymore than I did of my father.

A clear blue Sunday morning sky promised a beautiful day and it had arrived by eight o'clock. I arose much earlier than the previous morning and carried my coffee to the new deck off the kitchen. The air was brisk but light. No cloud disturbed the peaceful sun as it gently rose over the crest of Rocky Face. I had a sudden longing for a Sunday issue of the Flagstaff Times. Back there, the paper was as much a part of Sunday as was coffee.

All of a sudden, a tinny clang shattered the quiet morning. I jumped, startled, until I realized it was only the bell from the Zion Baptist Church down the road a few miles. I had heard that bell every Sunday until I left home for college and it still made me jump.

Suddenly weary, I wondered what to do with the day ahead. A notion crept into my head and although I tried to nudge it aside it grew and grew. I would go to church! For many people that would be the normal activity on Sunday morning.

However, in the area of religion, I was far from average or normal. I was neither an atheist nor even an agnostic. I had simply established in my mind over the years what my way of worship would be. And organized religion had no place in that worship. Religion seemed to me the most private of all things.

My parents had belonged to Calvary Free Will Baptist Church before I was born. They had never been avid churchgoers but maintained their membership over the years. I accompanied them to church as a small child and I believe that is what shaped my future outlook on religion.

The service would begin with a hymn sung by the entire congregation. If the occasion warranted, the selection might be a special one. There was "The Old Rugged Cross," for Easter, "Come Ye Faithful," for Thanksgiving, "Beautiful Star of Bethlehem," for Christmas, and if revival time was near, "Come Unto Me," or "Just As I Am." For the end of revival and baptizing, "Shall We Gather at the River."

Baptizing was held in a small pond in the creek behind the church. I feared being baptized. Although I was a good swimmer and could hold my breath under water for a long time, I dreaded the day when I might be coerced into allowing my body to be submerged while in the grasp of a preacher who had spent the entire previous week shouting and screaming, begging sinners to come forward and kneel at the altar in front of the pulpit.

My earliest memory of church was of the frenzied ravings of a succession of revival preachers. It would not be fair to refer to most of them as ministers; they preached! I recall quite well how I would hide my face in my mother's side and try to get away from the red-faced, screaming man in the pulpit.

Sometimes he would gradually calm down. Then, just as the fluttering in my stomach had begun to calm, he would raise his face to the ceiling, utter a few quiet words, and suddenly, with no warning, as if possessed by the very demon that he preached against, slap his Bible down on the podium.

The impact would ring out like a rifle shot and reverberate over the congregation. Sleepy old people would jerk their heads in unwilling admission of having been caught dozing. Some people kept their quiet placid expressions as my parents did. But some would nod their heads vigorously as if this action was proof that their preacher was filled and overflowed with the spirit and glory of the Almighty.

During revival, another preacher might add to the activities by walking up and down the aisles, stopping sometimes to choose a subject in the back rows where the "unsaved" and the backsliders sat. He would often exhaust his entire supply of tricks and still not persuade the person to take that long walk to the altar.

Other times, while the congregation turned to watch, a face would crumple and likely as not burst into sobs that the preacher interpreted as the pain of repentance. He would then lead them down the aisle, kneel with them at the altar, and make a plea to the congregation that "Every head be bowed and every eye closed while we make way for this soul to be offered up to Jesus."

The second ringing of the church bell brought me out of my reverie. Almost as suddenly as I had decided to go to church, I changed my mind. I knew there was no way to avoid seeing my father's grave. The tent would have been removed but the mound of flowers would remain until they had wilted and dried.

I had more to think about than my sorrow; now I must solve this puzzle of the events leading up to my father's death and just where Ed McKinney fitted into it.

Chapter Four

Wade Gwynn was twenty years my senior. I knew little about his personal life, just that he had been my father's attorney and friend for many years. His office was in a modest building on Main Street in the county seat of Athens.

I arrived early on Monday morning and sat quietly in the reception area while his secretary went to tell him I was there. Moments later he appeared in the door and motioned me to come in. I could tell by his expression that something had taken place in regards to Dad since I last saw him at the funeral.

I settled myself into a chair and faced him squarely. "What is it, Wade? What's happened since Friday?"

Elbows on desk, he touched the tips of his short stubby fingers together and took a long time to answer. When he did it was slow, careful, as if he wanted to make sure that he was saying exactly what was needed.

"Rachel, when I spoke to you at the funeral, I wanted to talk to you about your father's will. He made me the executor years ago and he never changed it. The will itself is simple.

"Everything goes to you, of course. I knew Paul might have some debts to be taken care of and I wanted to make sure that you knew what was involved."

Wade paused, as if to prepare himself for what came next.

"There will be the small debts, the usual ones, heating oil bill, electric, etc. I haven't had time to look specifically into those yet."

A frown creased his brow and his tone grew a bit guarded.

"I had a visitor first thing this morning. Ed McKinney."

I tried but could not keep the anxiety from my voice.

"What did he want to see you for? Surely not in connection with Dad?"

"Yes, I'm afraid so, Rachel. And it's no small matter, either. He informed me that Paul has a loan from First Colony Bank and no payment has been made in five months."

"But, surely there's enough in Dad's checking account to cover that?"

"I'm afraid not, Rachel. I called just a few minutes ago and found that his savings account has long been empty and the checking account had only five hundred and seventy-seven dollars in it."

I still didn't see the problem.

"Well, how much is the loan?"

Wade watched my face as he answered slowly, "Two hundred and thirty thousand dollars."

I know my eyes grew large; I felt them expand. My chest was uncomfortably tight and it occurred to me that maybe it had only sounded like Wade had said, "Two hundred and thirty thousand dollars." But he was; in fact, he repeated it several times.

"But, Wade," I stammered. "What…why…what did Dad need that kind of money for? Actually, why did he need to borrow money at all? He's always been pretty comfortable financially, at least as far as I've known!"

My mind was battered with wild questions. What in creation had Dad used that money for? When had he borrowed it? And, Ed McKinney again, appearing deeper and deeper into my father's affairs. Not so distant phrases echoed, Needed money…turned down by his own kin…

How long did I have? That seemed the only important thing at the moment. After a few seconds Wade answered somberly, "At the most, two weeks."

Two weeks to raise that kind of money. And the only kind of collateral Dad could have used for that size of loan was the land, of course. I swallowed, took a deep breath, and shoved the whole thing aside.

In true Scarlet O'Hara fashion I figured I would think about that later. Right now I wanted Wade to read the will and give me some idea of what was involved in settling the estate outside of the loan.

"I'll have to advertise," he said. "I'll put a notice in the Laurel Hill Gazette asking all debtors to come forward."

"Of course," I spoke bitterly, "the main debtor has already come forward."

"We'll work it out somehow," Wade answered. I knew he meant to be comforting but his words carried little conviction.

Suddenly I remembered the map and took it from my purse. Wade frowned as I unfolded and spread it on his desk.

"Here," I said. "This is what I wanted to ask you about. See these X's? Well, those are wooden stakes with orange plastic ribbon on them; they're driven in the ground at all these spots. What do you suppose they're for? I know they're not surveyor's markers because of the crazy pattern. No one would lay out a property line like that!"

Wade concentrated on the map. His eyes squinted as he traced the pattern with his forefinger.

"Uh-huh. Rachel, tell me, here, and there, are all these places steep? And these curves, are they around hills?"

"Yes," I said. "Yes to both questions, and that area that I circled there is the big level field at the foot of Rocky Face. Why? Is that important?"

"This may sound a bit far-fetched to you, Rachel, but my best guess is that someone has been laying out the boundaries for a ski slope!"

"But, that's impossible! That's still Dad's property and you know he would have said something to someone, you or Isaac or me. Wouldn't he, Wade?"

"It seems that way, Rachel. But, I don't believe you understand yet just how much Paul had changed."

At the look on my face his eyes softened and he said, "All right, I'll go to the Register of Deeds this afternoon and see if there's been any transfer of property.

"As for the other deal, the bank loan, if it comes down to the wire, you can always go to another bank and borrow to pay off this loan. At least that would give you some extra time."

There seemed nothing else to say. Wade walked me to the door and patted my shoulder, "Let me know if I can help in whatever you decide to do."

"Thanks, Wade."

I kissed his cheek and left. On my way to the car, halfway across the parking lot, the solution for paying off the loan came to me so clearly I wondered why it hadn't occurred to me immediately.

My inheritance! It would cover most of the amount and I knew that I could depend on David to help me raise the rest. I had only to say the word. I sighed in relief. That much was behind me. Now for the difficult part.

Paying off the loan was not going to solve the real problem, the enigma I had stumbled into. They were all connected, I was sure of that. The letters, the rumor that Dad had asked me for help and I had refused, the sale of the sawmill and the cattle, and the condition of the farm. Now this bank loan, and if Wade was correct, the outline of a ski slope on Dad's property.

Weaving it all together like spider webs, figuring into each crack and crevice was Ed McKinney. Somehow I had to find out what had been going on.

I made a mental note on the way home to call David and have him transfer the money from my account and the extra needed to the bank in Laurel Hill.

Then I remembered that Ed McKinney worked at First Colony. I did not want him to know that I could pay off the loan until I found out what was going on. I wanted him to think that the bank was going to foreclose and take Dad's property.

So I would have David transfer the money to another bank in Athens. Where the plans went from there I had no hint of but one thing for certain, I intended to find out where McKinney figured into all of this.

Chapter Five

Isaac was waiting for me when I reached the house. Knowing I loved good coffee, he had ground enough for a full pot and already had it on the stove. Also sensing how much at loose ends I would be, he had remembered my favorite lunch, cream of tomato soup and grilled cheese sandwiches.

"Figured you could use a little something," he said as he poured the soup into my bowl.

He sat down, his elbows on the table, his chin in both hands.

"You know, Rachel, I was thinking today. To lose somebody is bad. If they're older than you, it's not so hard to accept. But, to lose somebody that you've known since they were born, why, that's like losing a whole lifetime!"

For the first time since I had come home I broke down and sobbed. Isaac didn't say hush or don't cry, just stood with his arm around my shoulder until my tears faded away. Then he stated wryly that the grilled cheese was getting as tough as shoe leather and the percolator was fixing to boil over.

Silently I blessed him for his capacity to help me keep my emotions in check. I finished my lunch subdued and quiet. Isaac led the way out on the deck. Something occurred to me.

"Isaac, why did Dad have the sun porch replaced with this open deck? It's not very practical at all. Being on the southwest side of the house, it has to be too hot to sit here very much in the summer. I never noticed anything wrong with the porch. And when the glass was put in, it was a great place in the winter. Do you remember when Mom used to keep it full of Geraniums and Begonias all winter?"

"I don't really know, Rachel. He just took a notion I reckon. He used to talk that kind of thing over with me but I didn't know anything about this until I looked up one morning and the contractors already had the roof off the sun porch."

"I imagine it was expensive, wasn't it," I asked.

"Yeah, had to be. Its all built out of red cedar and you know what that costs. And they must have been working up here for three or four weeks."

"And what about the driveway, Isaac. And those drainage ditches in the orchard?"

"There was not one common sense reason to pave that driveway. Never had a mud-hole in it since the first time I drove over it more'n thirty-five years ago.

"That section of the orchard needed some drainage ditches, but not the kind they put in. Expensive, my God! He wouldn't let the County Soil Conservation Service help him at all. Ed McKinney hired a private firm out of Tennessee. And then, just stopped them at the road's edge. After a hard rain it's like a lake down there.

"Some time after that Paul decided he didn't want to bother with the orchard any more. So that was a lot of waste, too. But, the driveway was the most costly and the least needed. I never did understand that."

We were silent for a while. It was mid-afternoon and the sun was glaring over Rocky Face. With more composure than I felt, I related to Isaac what I had found out in Wade's office.

He showed very little surprise at the loan.

"I knowed he had to get some money somewhere. I don't know what he got for the sawmill and the cattle but for the last two years there's been no apple or tobacco crops, just no money coming in except his social security check and his military pension. But, I never suspected he'd borrowed that much."

Typically Isaac, he never asked what I was going to do about the loan. He just let me go on talking.

"About the markers, Isaac, have you seen any surveyors around or did Dad mention anything about it?"

"I never saw no surveyors around, but then, like I told you before, the driveway ain't the only way into that section of property. You could get in there easy enough from Hayes Road with a four-wheel drive.

"There are old roads where they hauled out logs so they wouldn't have to mess up this end of the property. You can't get in from the Parkway. The stone edging along that strip would stop a Sherman tank!

"And, no, Paul never said anything about selling any land! He might have got secretive and strange but let me tell you this! Paul Myers wasn't willingly fixing to sell none of his land and you can bet money on that!"

With that declaration, Isaac finished his coffee silently. I nibbled absently at the brown crust of my grilled cheese.

"You know I'm going to find out what's been happening here, don't you, Isaac?"

He nodded, his face grave and sad. Finally he said, "I hope so, Rachel. I surely do hope so."

I spent the rest of Monday wandering around the house, making lists of questions in need of answers. I could feel a familiar spark growing within me, one I had experienced many times before.

In its infancy it was only a tiny speck of anticipation at tackling an extremely difficult crossword or being able to put together a jigsaw puzzle quicker than anyone else and almost without thought.

Then, in my junior year of college, a roommate who lived in Ohio invited me to spend spring break with her family. Since she lived nearby, we visited the Great Serpent Mound, which was built by the ancient Adena Indians. We were walking around the mound when I suddenly became short of breath and had to fight an urge to run away. I did not even try to explain to my friend why we had to leave immediately because I didn't really know myself.

The strange feeling was magnified when David and I visited the area called Four Corners where Utah, Arizona, Nevada, and Colorado come together. We were exploring the Anasazi ruins on a bright summer's day with the temperatures in the seventies.

We climbed the ladder to the top and David walked through one of the strange doorways that are wide at the top, narrow at the bottom, while I stood looking down into one of the ceremonial Kivas.

Suddenly I shuddered as a chill encompassed my entire body and I felt possessed by an uncontrollable urge to speak, to say something. It was not a déjà vu thing, no, I think I've been here before, no delusional vision. And, just as it had been at the Snake Mound, I was unable to explain what I felt. I refused to acknowledge the occurrences as anything except the normal response to an enigma.

Then, in the nursing home where I worked, a nursing supervisor came to me one day and informed me of a situation where an elderly, terminal patient was being upset by his niece. The niece had been observed trying to convince the elderly man to sign a piece of paper. The supervisor had learned from the patient's attorney that his ironclad will left everything to various foundations and endowments. So, what did the niece want?

For the first time in my life, I felt simple curiosity grow into an almost irrational desire to find the answer. After investigating for weeks, I learned that the old man's late wife had owned an obscure piece of property that he had apparently forgotten about. Because it did not appear specifically in his will, the niece was hoping to have it signed over to her. More digging revealed that the property joined an area that was shortly to become an exclusive golfing community development and the only natural water source for nearly twenty miles was in the middle of the thirty-acre tract.

That was the first time I realized that the reason I had enjoyed writing papers in college was because the assignments were like puzzles to be reconstructed with various pieces of research.

And, I finally admitted to myself that, all vanity aside, I had a gift for synthesizing things and putting them in their proper places almost without thinking.

Also, I had played the cello since high school and I knew that its great attraction for me was in the mystery of finding the exact movement of the bow across the strings to produce the desired sound. I was part of an ensemble that played mostly for nursing homes and at charity events where we nearly always performed old familiar pieces.

On my own I was drawn to odd and difficult music that might take me hours to master even a small portion of a composition. I had long since stopped trying to explain to anyone, David included, my fascination for the enigmatic, the mysterious, the seemingly unfathomable.

Well, there was no way to tell whether any part of past experiences would help me to learn what had happened to my father, but at least I was certain of my own tenacity and knew that I would not stop until I was satisfied.

I called Wade Gwynn and asked him to find out how much it cost Dad to pave the driveway, dig the ditches, and have the barn and deck built. I would try to find out how much Dad had gotten for the cattle and the sawmill.

The price of cattle was simple to come by. I called the livestock market in Athens and after I convinced them I was who I said I was, they had the information for me within minutes.

"Yes, Miss Myers, we have the information you wanted. It came to twelve thousand dollars."

I wrote down the exact amount and asked if it had been sent to my father or deposited directly in the bank.

"We sent it directly to Mr. Myers. But, you know, why... this is very unusual! There's a note attached to this file that says we've contacted Mr. Myers by mail three times to ask him to deposit that check so we can keep our accounts in order!"

I was astounded!

"You mean that check has never been cashed?"

"No, Ma-am, I mean, yes Ma-am, that's exactly what I mean."

The voice continued, "We'd certainly appreciate your remedying the situation if you can. Of course, if the check has been lost, we can easily issue a new one for Mr. Myers. He's a good customer, done business with us for years."

I thanked her and hung up. Well, my quest for the answer to one question simply resulted in another. Where was that check? Had it been misplaced or deliberately destroyed?

I decided to search for it later and flipped through the papers in the drawer under the telephone hoping to find some company name that looked as if it would be a purchaser of sawmill equipment.

Finally, a ragged envelope stuck between two sheets of coffee stained paper. Townsend Bros. Logging Company, Roanoke, Virginia and a telephone number. I dialed immediately with trembling fingers.

A gruff voice answered and before I could speak stated he was not the secretary, she was out at the moment.

I swallowed and tried to steady my voice.

"I'm trying to find out what your company paid Mr. Paul Myers for some sawmill equipment about nine months ago."

His voice dropped.

"And who wants to know, IRS?"

"No," I said quickly, "I do. I'm his daughter. My father…died a few days ago and I'm trying to put his business affairs in order."

"In that case, sure, why not? Just take a minute."

Before my thoughts could shift to another subject, he was back.

"Ah, Miss Myers? Yeah, I've got that file right here. We paid him sixty-eight thousand for everything he had. Strange thing though. Says here the check has never been deposited. You know, if you'll get the probate lawyer to write to us, we'll be glad to issue a new one. Just send…"

Same story. Why had my father not deposited those checks? Had he become that absent minded? If so, Isaac would surely have known and mentioned it to me.

I took coffee and a sweet roll out to the deck and sat in the twilight. If Isaac were here, he'd chide me for not eating a real supper but food was far from first on my priority list at the moment. A melancholy settled over me as I stared at the horizon. As darkness fell, security lights appeared, twinkling like stars on the mountainsides, rendering land and sky almost indistinguishable.

A whip-or-will began to call very softly from somewhere down the ridge. Lord, how long had it been since I had heard a whip-or-will? Ten, twelve years, I supposed. The call became clearer, closer, and then an answer from only a short distance away. "Whip-or-will, whip-or-will." A perfect echo if one did not know that it was two birds calling and answering each other.

Twilight faded slowly into darkness. I sat there, reluctant to go inside, still trying to grasp the true significance of the undeposited checks and all the other questions. Why had all this happened? Could I have prevented it if I had been there?

But, I told myself, Dad would have been the first one to say I had my own life to live. Isaac had been there but had been powerless to make any difference.

My thoughts turned entirely to Ed McKinney. He was not a complete stranger to me. He had moved to Laurel Hill when I was just a teenager. He was unmarried and quite a few years older than I, which might put his age at about 45, I supposed. I knew him the way many people knew a stranger who moved into a small mountain community, just enough to say a casual hello.

How then had the relationship between Dad and McKinney begun? From what little I could remember about him, he was not a very likely candidate for Dad to have taken into his personal confidences. Isaac said McKinney started coming to see Dad just a while after my last visit, nearly two years before.

He surely must have gained my father's trust completely. Otherwise, Dad would never have agreed to let Mrs. Campbell go. She had been with him for so long, nearly five years, ever since his sight had taken the last turn for the worse.

"Well," I contemplated. "There's a thought."

I would try to find out where Mrs. Campbell was in Florida. Knowing her free-speaking nature, I was sure she wouldn't hesitate to tell me all she knew about the situation.

Sleep came slowly that night. The wind blew hard and the house quivered. I lay wide-eyed, staring into the darkness. Somewhere a loose board banged. I pulled my pillow around my head to muffle the sound but I could hear it yet, an eerie, baleful sound.

When I finally drifted off, I dreamed of David walking beside me in a beautiful flower garden. As we went deeper into the garden, pieces of rusty saw blades lay haphazardly over the flowers and my arms were not long enough to reach down to move them aside. Cows grazed, eating only the blossoms, ignoring the grass. I turned to protest to David, to ask his help.

Although he still wore the same clothing, his face had changed to that of Ed McKinney. The face was fuzzy, out of focus, as if I were looking through a maladjusted camera lens. I was terrified and tried to run away but could not move my feet.

In slow motion, McKinney waved a check in each hand. His mouth spat words in singsong.

"Thirty-thousand whip-or-wills, thirty-thousand whip-or-wills."

Over and over and over with his voice growing louder and his movements growing more sluggish. My feet were stuck fast, I could not move; my body, my mind was growing larger, inflating, any moment I would burst!

Suddenly I was sitting up in bed, gasping for air. My body was drenched in a cold sweat and my heart pounded fiercely against my ribs. I stared at a rectangle of pale, early morning sky. The ballerina curtains moved slightly in front of the open window.

I lay trying to lull myself into sleep again. A whip-or-will called from the oak tree behind the house. I finally drifted off, not having heard whether or not it received an answer.

Chapter Six

"Wade, that adds up to nearly two hundred and fifty thousand dollars!"

"You get an A-plus on your math. That's what my calculations come to. To be exact, two hundred and forty-eight thousand, nine hundred and seventy-six dollars. Sorry, Rachel, can you hold on for a sec?"

I was stunned into a total silence. Although there had been no way to avoid accepting the fact that Dad had spent a lot of money, I had harbored a faint hope that some secret account would turn up and would yield at least part of the money from the loan.

"Rachel, are you still there, Rachel?"

Wade sounded a bit worried.

"Yes," I said. "Yes, I'm here."

It just took me a few moments to digest this new addition to the puzzle.

"Wade, why do you think Dad spent that money? Or borrowed it in the first place? You know, not a single thing he spent it for was even vaguely necessary.

"That metal barn was built weeks after the last of his cattle were sold. It's never been used.

"And paving a driveway the length of his was a luxury that someone like Dad could never afford.

"And those drainage ditches. It just doesn't add up, Wade.

"How could someone as level headed as Dad do something like this? He had to have a lot of encouragement and it seems to me that only one person was in a position to give him that!"

Anger rose inside of me until my face burned. Wade answered quickly.

"Rachel, I've already concluded that point. What I can't figure out is what I'm sure you've already thought of: what Ed McKinney could possibly gain from influencing your father to borrow and spend that money.

"There's no question that it was legal to the letter, the loan, the contracts for all the work, everything. McKinney certainly never profited from any of that, that is, unless it's mighty well hidden. And if the loan is defaulted on and the bank forecloses, why, the property would go to the bank to dispose of. I can't see McKinney coming up with that kind of money."

"Wade," I said, my spirits dropping, "there's more all the time I don't understand. I wish to God I had been here. Maybe I could have kept all of this from happening. Maybe Dad would still be alive."

"Rachel, you know Paul wouldn't have wanted that. He was so proud of you. And he always believed that people should control their own lives."

"Yeah, well, it seems he didn't control his own life very well during the past couple of years."

Wade was silent. I said goodbye and hung up.

The coffee in my cup was cold and bitter. I poured it down the sink and helped myself to another. I barely heard the lock turn in the kitchen door, so deeply I was into my thoughts.

"Morning, Rachel. Who plowed them furrows in your brow?"

Without acknowledging his question, I asked, "Isaac, tell me about the tobacco allotment. When did Dad decide to stop leasing it out?"

"As you already know, we hadn't raised any burley for about ten years ourselves. It cut down too much on what was to be made off of it, hiring people to pull plants, set, weed, hoe and sucker. I guess we could've stayed with it but with Paul's sight….

"And it's hard anymore to find somebody that knows how to cut and stake it. Didn't seem like there was anybody left that knowed how to grade it when it came into case around Christmas time."

Isaac's voice trailed off. I could almost see the whole process taking place in his mind.

"You don't have to tell me all that, Isaac. If you recall, I was a pretty good tobacco hand myself!"

His voice was distant as though his own thoughts were all he could hear. Then he collected himself.

"What you asked about…. Paul just told me two years ago, in February, I guess it was, that he would talk to Jud Critcher about the lease on the allotment that spring.

"Of course, I didn't say anything. It was Paul's business and I just figured he was trying to get a bit more into doing things for himself. But, later on, up in May, way after planting time, I saw Jud down to the feed store and he asked me why Paul hadn't wanted to lease his allotment out that year.

"That was the first I had heard about it. See, when Jud leased it he sometimes grew the crop on his own land. That's why, when the land laid empty in the spring, I didn't think anything of it. I just thought that Jud had decided to raise it over on his place."

Suddenly, out of nowhere, for the first time, I wanted to hear about Dad's death.

"Isaac," I begged quietly, "tell me. Tell me about when you found Dad. Please, I need to know."

I knew from what he had already told me that he was the one who found my father that morning. Until now, I had not had the courage or the inclination to ask about it.

Now I wanted, no, needed to know. Perhaps it was my growing sense of guilt for not being there; perhaps because the hurt was beginning to ease and I felt some masochistic need to continue suffering. Anyway, I needed to know.

Isaac began.

"Not a whole lot to tell, really. I just came up here like I'd done every morning for six or seven years, I reckon. Your dad and me, we'd just sit here and drink coffee and talk. Use to talk about what he wanted me to do that day but we hadn't done that for a long time.

"Anyway, I unlocked the kitchen door. Sometimes Paul would already be up. You'd be surprised what he could still do for himself, blindness or no. He could make a pot of coffee as well as I could. Near about as fast, too. He never tried much cooking but that was okay. At breakfast he usually just ate cornflakes or something like that.

"He always turned on the radio, though. He kept up with the farm news. And he liked that new station out of Tennessee that played old country music."

I already knew everything that Isaac was saying, but I let him take his time getting to what I wanted to hear. His eyes were moist and sad.

"Like I said, I came in here and everything seemed a bit strange, no coffee started and no radio playing. I thought he must be still in bed. He hadn't been sleeping well for a long time.

"I started the coffee and set down a minute at this table and then decided to go into the den and turn on the television to one of them news shows until Paul got up. Soon as I started through the dining room, I saw him."

Isaac stopped and I was afraid he wouldn't go on so I stayed quiet. He ran his hand down over his face, that familiar gesture I had seen a thousand times.

"He was just laying there beside the china cabinet, all stretched out. One arm was over his head like he was reaching for something. I knowed in my heart it wasn't no use but I looked on top of the cabinet for his pills. They wasn't there so I tried to rouse him. Wasn't no use of that neither. He was already cold.

"Doc Hartley said that Paul had been dead for over seven hours. I thought about that later. Felt awful, knowing that while I was laying there close by, sound asleep in my bed, the best man I ever knowed was up here dying. Well, that's all there was to it. Doc Hartley took care of the calling that needed to be done. I was a might confused myself."

A single tear had escaped and ran down his cheek. He sniffed loudly and cleared his throat.

"That what you wanted to hear?"

I could not answer, only nodded. My heart was heavy but suddenly a notion stirred in my head. It took me a few moments to identify what it was.

"Isaac, did you ever find Dad's pills?"

He looked at me, his bland expression giving his opinion of the inanity of my question.

"Well, no. There wasn't no need to look for them with him already stone cold dead!"

I winced at his choice of words but went on with my inquiry.

"Didn't you tell me that Dad always kept his pills on the top of that cabinet?"

"Yeah, the ones he took when he felt an attack coming on. The ones he took every day he kept in the medicine cabinet. They're right there where they belong. It's the others that are missing."

"Then, why didn't you question why they weren't there, Isaac?"

"Like I said before, Rachel, Paul was gone and I wasn't thinking too straight. And there were more important things to take care of."

"Isaac," I said while trying to keep the suspicion in my voice to a minimum. "What if Dad got to where his pills were supposed to be and then died because they weren't there? If somebody moved them, that would almost be tantamount to murder, wouldn't it?"

The silence was heavy. Finally he said, "Surely you wouldn't be thinking that I moved them pills, would you?"

I reached for his weathered hand and held it in both of mine.

"Oh no, Isaac, never! That's not what I meant at all. But, think about it. If Dad hadn't gotten to where he kept his pills, it wouldn't matter if they were there or not. But, if he reached that cabinet and they'd been moved..."

My voiced trailed off and we were both very quiet for a while.

"Isaac, I've got it. I knew there was something – what you said when I asked you about the letters from me, don't you remember?"

He nodded, memory brightening his blue eyes.

"Yeah, I reckon I do recall. The morning before he died when I was looking for that shed key. Nothing was there except Paul's little bottle of heart pills and thinking that the key might have fallen down behind, I pulled the cabinet out and that's when them letters from you fell to the floor. Or what was supposed to be letters, anyway."

I nearly shouted in jubilant exasperation.

"Isaac, do you still not see what I'm getting at? The pills were there the day before Dad died. Why should they not have been there when he needed them that night? Oh, come on, let's look, let's see if we can find that bottle right now!"

For nearly an hour we looked. No drawer or enclosed space went unsearched. We even dipped under sofa cushions and behind dust-laden books in the den.

When we were almost ready to give up, I found the small prescription bottle, half full of tiny white pills. It was in the pantry, all the way back in the corner behind a box of oatmeal. Certainly out of reach of a blind person, or anyone needing them in an emergency. The label read Trinitrin: take 1 tablet under tongue as directed for pain.

Isaac's face was grave and he remained silent at the appearance of the bottle. I knew what he was thinking because I was thinking the same thing. The bottle had been deliberately hidden in the pantry. He hadn't put it there, Mrs. Campbell obviously hadn't, since she had been gone for two months, so that left only one person in the house frequently enough to know where the bottle was kept and what it was for.

My mind rebelled, would not even let me think the name. The implication just added to the horrible question of why? Why would anyone who had professed to be a good friend to Dad perform such a cruel act? My mind struggled helplessly searching for some answer to it all.

Suddenly, I longed for David, for his shoulder, his arms, his warmth and his ability to make even the worst situations seem better.

"So, what do we do about this?"

My brain reacted slowly to Isaac's question.

"I don't know. I don't know what we can do. I'll talk to Wade Gwynn and see what he suggests. I don't think we have enough to go on to justify involving anyone else right now."

There was a finality about our discovery, as if there was just nothing else to say, at least for the time being. Isaac stood up to leave and I noticed for the first time the slight stoop in his thin shoulders. He patted my hand but did not speak as he made his way to the door.

"Isaac!" I jumped up, almost upsetting my chair. "Was anyone here with Dad that night, I mean earlier in the evening?"

"I really don't know, Honey. I left at five o'clock that afternoon to help George Willis take a load of cows over to the other side of Athens. Must have been eleven or after by the time I got back. The house was dark, like

Paul had already gone to bed. Which he usually had by that time."

"But there could have been someone here earlier?"

"I reckon so. But, I don't know how you'd ever find out for sure."

He left then and I watched him go down the hill, hands clasped behind his back.

"He's lost as much as I have," I thought, as he disappeared through his front door.

I sat back down and began to try to figure out how to go about learning if anyone had seen Dad that afternoon or evening. I turned loose my basically logical mind and, as Isaac would say, "Had a go round at it." I grabbed pen and paper. Things written down were tangible, easier to grasp.

First, who might have come to the house on a Tuesday, late afternoon or evening? I considered all the deliveries that might have been made. Mail: too late in the day. Electric meter: wrong time of the month. Salesman: assuming one might come that late in the day, impossible to trace.

Suddenly I shivered, a combination of the nature of my speculations and the temperature. The sun had gone behind a cloud and in the mountains that means a drop in the mercury. Only after the furnace thermostat clicked as I pushed it up to seventy, did I remember. I searched frantically through a drawer for a yellow slip of paper that I had found on the counter when I first entered the house.

I found it, an oil bill for 250 gallons of heating oil at two dollars and ninety-four cents per gallon, total seven hundred and thirty-five dollars. The most important item on the bill was the date. October 17, 2005.

My father had died that night around eleven o'clock.. I bit my lip and tried to stifle what I knew was premature optimism.

"I must not let myself get too hopeful. This doesn't mean he was here in the evening. It could have been first thing that morning."

My hands trembled as I dialed the number and asked to speak to delivery person twenty-two. An androgynous voice said, "Number twenty-two is out on delivery but if you'll leave your number, please?"

The sun had begun to sink when the telephone rang. Wade wanted to let me know that there had been no transfer of property belonging to my father. I thanked him and put that information aside. It paled in comparison to my discovery of the misplaced bottle of pills. I started to tell Wade about that and ask his advice but thought better of it. I would wait until I heard from the oil delivery person. Then I would take it from there.

I was almost ready to climb into a hot bath, certain that it was too late for the oil truck driver to call, when the phone rang. I grabbed the hall extension.

"Hello?"

"Yes, hello. This is Amy Burgess."

Puzzled, I said, "How can I help you?"

"I'm with Connard Oil," she said. "Is this Rachel Myers?"

I thanked her while trying to keep the surprise at her gender out of my voice. My heart thumped wildly.

"Yes, yes, it is. Thanks for returning my call. What I need to know, is there any way to find out what time you delivered oil to my father, Paul Myers, last week on the seventeenth?"

"Sure, it's right here." There was a slight pause and the sound of shuffling papers. "Eight o'clock or to be exact, seven fifty five. See, I'm the newest employee so I drive one of the older trucks that only prints out how much oil has been pumped so I have to keep my own time sheet and turn a copy in at the end of each day. I don't usually deliver that late but this time of year everybody wants their tanks filled."

Her voice grew softer. "Oh, yeah, I'm sorry to hear about your Dad. He was a nice guy."

"Thank you," I answered hastily, "but, also, do you remember, was anyone there at my father's house that evening?"

"Well," she said carefully, " I couldn't swear that there was any one person there. I mean, I never saw anyone. I just tucked my bill into the storm door like always. But, Ed McKinney's car was there, if that's any help."

My heart leapt and I tried hard to keep the quiver out of my voice.

"How can you be so sure it was Ed McKinney's car if you didn't see him?"

"Well, mainly because he drives a silver Corvette with a red racing stripe down the side. And you can bet there's not another car like that here in Laurel Hill!"

I skipped the bath, and dinner, making do with just a glass of milk. It was pitch dark but I decided to walk down and tell Isaac about this new bit of information. There were no lights visible in his house but I knew the room that served as his kitchen and den was at the front so I would not be able to see the light from my yard. I walked slowly, contemplating the new development and what it implied.

I might be giving it more importance than it deserved but, since Ed McKinney had been there that evening, there was a chance I was right. He could have hidden the bottle of pills.

Except, and this was a gigantic except, he couldn't possibly have known that Dad would need them that night. They were Trinitrin to be taken only when he felt an attack of Angina coming on. So how could anyone anticipate a thing like that?

Isaac was not at home. Long shadows from tall poplars in front of his house cast dark bars across his door as if to ward off anyone who might intrude while he was out.

I would have to wait until morning. So, I'd try to get some sleep and be ready for tomorrow. The passion to prove that all was not as it appeared in my father's death, yes, and for months before his death, burned more furiously inside me with every hour that passed.

The whip-or-wills called again that night but I was almost oblivious to anything but my own thoughts. I tried to squelch them because I knew from experience that if my mind were too active, sleep would be long in coming. I fought an inclination to get up and look for a cigarette, something I hadn't had for years.

I got up and instead of cigarettes, found an unopened bottle of wine with a North Carolina label. Must have been a gift. Dad never drank wine, only occasionally straight whiskey, preferably home grown. The wine was soft, and turned my mind toward thoughts of David. Soaring, sweet, dipping low, gently swinging, his face appeared before me, not changing this time. After all, these thoughts, these memories were real, not a dream. David…David.

Chapter Seven

The whip-or-will did not disturb me that night and the next morning I awoke slowly from troubled dreams of Flagstaff. I became aware of the dawn through half-open eyes. I had slid down in the bed and my feet were pressed lightly against the foot-board. I could almost hear my mother padding about the kitchen, humming and rattling pots and pans.

I tried to recall what had awakened me but my mind found only opalescent fragments. I remembered vaguely a soft beach breeze and the pounding surf. But the rest was lost and now the responsibility of the new day pressed upon me.

My head ached, probably from the lack of dinner and an over-indulgence of wine just before going to bed. A multitude of different thoughts blended with the pain. The empty wine glass sat on the nightstand, a tiny syrupy gold puddle in the bottom.

Something made me want to stay in my bed instead of rising to meet the day. I tried a trick from my childhood. If I pulled the cover over my head and closed my eyes for long enough, the day would pass and I could go back to sleep and wake up the next morning having missed a dreaded algebra test or dissection in biology lab or anything else bad or painful. It didn't work. It never had.

I struggled to the bathroom for aspirin and a wet cloth for my aching head. A swallow of water to wash down the aspirin caused a wave of nausea, even though the water was clean and cold. Coffee didn't sound much better but I knew it would help the ache that pounded relentlessly in my temples. I put on the coffeepot and then noticed that I had left out all the bits of paper from the drawer where I had found the heating oil bill the night before.

On the bottom of the stack was a newspaper clipping, several months old, about a new county ordinance governing the dumping of trash along public roadsides. The face in the faded photograph jumped out at me. My high school friend, Stephen Phillips, "Spud" for short!

"How about that," I thought. "Spud a county planner."

I read the entire article through bleary eyes. One sentence caught my attention.

Phillips, an engineer with Rogers Engineering and Surveying before completing his degree in urban planning at Chapel Hill, states that the ordinance applies countywide and will be strictly enforced.

In a flash it was obvious that this was the possible solution to the last piece of the puzzle I must find before I confronted McKinney. I was a bit taken aback by my thoughts. I had not consciously contemplated going to face him.

But now I knew I would as soon as I discovered if he had anything to do with the markers. And that's where my old friend "Spud" might help!

I tried to busy myself with breakfast to pass the next half hour. Several times I reached for the telephone although I knew county offices did not open until eight o'clock.

When the digital clock on the stove said four minutes past eight, I dialed.

"Stephen Phillips. Can I help you?"

I had thought a receptionist would answer and before I could collect myself I blurted out, "Spud?"

His voice changed from business to a more personal tone.

"Yeah, who's this?"

"Ah...Stephen, it's Rachel, Rachel Myers."

"Rachel? Hey, Rachel, how are you? Where are you? Hey, it's good to hear from you. Its been forever..."

I hesitated; suddenly and atypically shy, I apologized.

"I'm sorry, I didn't intend to call you Spud. It's just that I thought someone else would answer the phone and when I heard your voice, I thought Spud and not Stephen."

"That's all right, Rachel, that's just fine," he said, seeming to catch the tenseness in my voice. "When we were kids, not many people even knew my name was Stephen. I was Spud to everyone."

"Spud... Stephen, I don't suppose you heard about Dad. He died last week... heart attack. That's why I'm home."

A slight pause and then he answered.

"No, I hadn't heard, Rachel. I've been out of town since last Tuesday for a conference. Just got in late last night. I'm really sorry to hear that. Your dad was a great guy. Of course, you know that. He was the only person in Laurel Hill who would trust us kids with his horse and wagon for a hayride."

A silence followed that I finally broke.

"Spud, I need help. See, there're a lot of things that have happened over the past two years that I can't figure out. In fact, I'm not even sure about Dad's death. I mean, whether or not a heart attack was all there was to it. Look, I can't explain now but I promise I will later if you'll look into something for me."

"Nothing's too good for the first girl I ever kissed," he kidded. "Just name it, Rachel."

I told him all about the markers on Dad's property but only a little about the rest. He promised to look into it right away and get back to me as soon as he learned anything definite.

But before he hung up he asked, "You did say Rachel Myers, didn't you? Good, that gives us something else to talk about."

I had intended to make an appointment to see Dr. Hartley but when his receptionist answered, I asked if you was possible to speak with him.

"I'll ask," she said. And then, "Hold on just a minute, Ms. Myers. He'll be right with you."

Dr. Hartley expressed his condolences about my father and then asked how he could help me. I explained the situation, mostly about the hidden pills.

"What I really want to understand is, Dr. Hartley, could Dad have died as a direct result of not having the Trinitin when he needed it?"

"Rachel, I wish I could answer that with some certainty but I can't. Paul had had Angina for about four years and you've probably guessed by now that he didn't want you to know how serious it was. I tried but obviously I wasn't successful in changing his mind about that. He was taking a calcium channel blocker that seemed to be doing a pretty good job of controlling his blood pressure. The Trinitrin, or nitroglycerin as it's generically called, was for sudden attacks of chest pain, nausea, and dizziness.

"About the most I can say, and this is just my personal opinion, you understand, is that if he was having a bad episode and went to get his medicine and couldn't find it, the panic he would likely have experienced might just have been enough to cause a fatal heart attack. But, as I said before, we just can't know that with any viable degree of certainty."

Isaac came in just after I hung up. Suddenly I thought of how it would be for him after I left. There would be no reason for him to open that kitchen door every morning to see if things were all right the way he had done with Dad for so many years. I pushed the thought away. I could not dwell on that with so much else happening. He helped himself to coffee and sat down across the table.

"I came down to see you last night," I said. "Had some news for you but you must have been out carousing around."

"Yeah," he answered, failing to maintain his usual serious expression. "You know just about how much carousing I do. Jack Whaley stopped by to see if I wanted to ride over to Athens to a Soil Conservation meeting. What was the news?"

"Well, I found out that McKinney was here the evening before Dad died."

I went on to tell him about my conversation with the oil truck driver and that I had talked with Doctor Hartley and Stephen Phillips.

"Also, Wade Gwynn called to say that there'd been no transfer of title on any of Dad's property."

Isaac studied this for a moment, unsurprised, then asked, "Well, what do you reckon that means?"

"I know what it means to me," I said. "It means as soon as I find out if Ed McKinney had anything to do with those markers, I'm going to see him.

"Doesn't it seem strange to you that since he was supposed to be such a good friend to Dad, that he wasn't at the funeral and hasn't been around to offer his condolences?"

"Nothing strange about it to me," Isaac said. "Ed McKinney knows I'd just as soon he kept himself away from here."

He drained his coffee cup and rinsed it out. "Where's your breakfast?"

"I'm not really hungry right now, Isaac," I said, but to appease him, "I'll have something later in the morning."

"You'd best keep up your strength," he warned as he left. "Sometimes this kind of situation takes more energy than hard labor."

I stayed close to the phone, hoping Spud would call soon. Stephen "Spud..." he had been about the nicest boy all the way through school. And he obviously hadn't changed. The hayrides he had spoken of, class picnics, snow sledding, all things I hadn't thought of in years.

Stephen, Donna Matheson and I had been the "Three Mountaineers" from the time we started first grade until we mounted the stage in cap and gown to receive our high school diplomas. I was the quieter one, Stephen the sensible and reliable, and Donna the vivacious and daring.

Through all our youth we met the odds head-on, whatever they were and many times we won out of sheer persistence, egged on by each other. Between the three of us we seemed to possess the combination of every quality one needed to get along. In schoolwork or summer adventures, we created our own world.

Then, along about ninth grade, romance reared its confusing head. It didn't take long for the matter to settle itself. Donna was not one to be tied to only one fellow, no matter how nice he was. Her plans were too full of excitement and glamour to allow them to be dulled by a future glimpse of marriage, babies and all that goes hand in hand with those two.

So naturally, Stephen and I became a twosome while Donna's eyes overflowed with stardust. She didn't complain when he and I started to spend time together, as long as we didn't shut her out entirely. We never tried to; she was too much fun.

She could add more to a party with one toss of her honey blond hair than a gym full of cheerleaders. She would flutter her long dark lashes over crystal blue eyes and take the heart of an innocent young freshman in ten seconds flat while Stephen and I looked on. It was a game to her, how quickly she could add another link to her chain of captive hearts. But, in her defense, she was never cruel, and she remained friends with most of them after she moved on to the next.

Then, college divided us, sent us scurrying off in different directions in search of our futures. Donna went to Business College and of course, business turned out to be glamorous and exciting just as she had always planned. She became a flight attendant for a major airline and jetted all over the world sending back postcards filled with news flashes about this beautiful country, that gorgeous man, and all the celebrities she chanced to meet.

Finally, Mr. Right flew into her life, literally. He was a pilot with the top competitor of the airline she worked for. They had an eventful, and I'm sure, exciting but very brief marriage. On one of my trips home, Dad said that someone had told him that Donna's gorgeous pilot had gorgeous flight attendants all around the world that he couldn't give up just because he happened to be married.

So, Donna spent a few hours mourning her unfortunate situation, then settled even more comfortably back into her profession. She finally got into the real glamour part that she had been hoping for all along. She made television commercials for the airline.

The last time I heard from her she was director of public relations for the airline's southeastern district and living the high life in Miami, Florida. I was sure she was excellent at her job. Relating had always been her forte.

Chapter Eight

My thoughts had strayed way too far from the present situation. To kill some time, I decided to go for another ride on Stayman. The early morning was superb. There had been a light rain during the night and the trees and bushes and even the weeds sparkled cleanly in the sunlight as if the whole world had been laundered and hung out to dry.

I knew if I was not in the house Stephen would call back later. Besides, it might take him all day, or longer, to find out what I wanted to know. He couldn't just completely put his job aside to work for me.

I avoided the section of land where the markers were and went in the opposite direction. The trail was narrower but still clear. It wound its way around clumps of trees and boulders to the top of a mountain on which rested a giant rock cliff. As far back as anyone knew it had been called Pigeon Crest. During the late eighteen hundreds passenger pigeons had roosted on this mountain in numbers inconceivable to anyone who had never seen them.

My mother had told me that as a young girl she had known an elderly woman who had actually seen the pigeons. She spoke of the sky darkening, the sun completely blocked as if by a thundercloud when the pigeons would fly in to roost on the cliff.

The fact that the bird had been extinct for nearly a century added poignancy to the story and because of that, the mountain had always held a mystique for me. Almost anything one runs out of can be replaced, except a living species. There is a fearsome sadness in the fact that no human from now on through eternity will ever look on that species alive again.

The top of Pigeon Crest offered a beautiful view of the surrounding country. An old legend said that five states could be seen from the top: Tennessee, South Carolina, Virginia, Georgia and Kentucky. I had never heard of it being proven but as I looked out across the Blue Ridge it was not difficult to believe.

The mountains, true to their name, crested in innumerable layers, the closer ones a dark bright blue, the further ones an indefinite fuzzy blue as if viewed through a mist. Actually, the color was supposed to come from a vapor that rose from all the pine trees. I preferred to think of it as their actual color.

I dismounted and left Stayman grazing on a sparse patch of grass between two ancient crabapple trees. Out on the edges of the cliff I tossed down pieces of bark and sticks and wondered if I dropped a tissue, would it float back up as it was reputed to do at the Blowing Rock? I substituted a large dry leaf but it kept going down, floating slowly, until it finally reached bottom.

From where I sat I could see rooflines and other evidence of houses built in the most unlikely places. Isaac had enlightened me about the rise in the tourist population in the past ten years. It had doubled several times over.

And it was a year round business now, unlike decades before when there were only 'summer folk.' The majority then were retirees seeking the peace and quiet of the area for a few weeks in the summer. Now tourism was big business.

Huge corporations had bought up tracts of mountain land, using the most suitable parts for ski slopes. Exclusive housing and golf courses covered the remainder. In my ignorance, I had assumed that it was necessarily good for the area, bringing money and jobs where there had been little of either in the past.

Isaac saw it from a different perspective. Steadily rising property taxes. Young people, natives of the area, unable to pay the skyrocketing prices for an acre or less on which to build a home. Coming from an area as expensive as Flagstaff, I was shocked to hear the average price of an acre of land. And of course, the closer to the resorts, the more expensive it became.

I had to concede that it had changed life in the area, one of the most obvious changes being increased amount of traffic on the narrow crooked two-lane mountain roads. Whether the growth was for the better, I supposed depended upon a person's viewpoint. Certainly, to look out on what was once a pristine expanse and see evidence of houses that dotted every mountainside was a bit unsettling.

Another curiosity that I would have to quiz Isaac about was the sides of tall mountains entirely void of trees. The areas were too completely cleared to be logging sites and surely no crops could be grown on such steep land.

I stood for a while and watched as a large turkey buzzard circled above one of the empty places. Before long several others had joined him but I was too far away to see what had attracted them. Next time I would look for binoculars before riding out.

Stayman picked his way carefully back down the mountain. I felt a bit nostalgic, a bit sad. But that feeling vanished when we reached the bottom of the hill and I let Stayman break into a slow smooth canter. No experience had ever filled my body or soul with pure unadulterated freedom like a good gallop on horseback. Looking down between Stayman's ears, the very earth seemed to part and give way for us. He was panting slightly when we reached the barn. I unsaddled and walked him dry.

"Don't tell Isaac about that run, old boy. He thinks we're both too old and out of shape!"

He blew softly as if to agree and trotted away to roll in the dry dirt of his favorite wallow.

Before I reached the house, I realized that I had not heeded Isaac's direction about breakfast. I was hungry and my knees were weak. The refrigerator yielded eggs, cheese, ham and a small jar of mushrooms, the perfect ingredients for an omelet. I ate my fill and hoped that Isaac would return in time to eat the rest before it grew cold.

After I thought about it, though, I decided not, after all. Isaac was partial to plain foods. Barker enjoyed the remainder of the omelet, wagging his bushy tail as if to let me know that his tastes were far more advanced than some.

It was almost five o'clock that afternoon when the telephone rang. The sound was startling even though I was expecting it. I hesitated, wondering if I really wanted to hear whatever Spud had found out. Another shrill ring and I spoke into the receiver, "Hello?"

"Hello, Rachel, it's Stephen. Look, I'm sorry it took this long to get back to you. I got tied up with some business about zoning regulations even though we don't have them here yet. Then it was more complicated finding out who had done the surveying than I thought it would be."

I interrupted, "Then, it's actually been surveyed, not just marked?"

"You bet it has. You just weren't out near the property lines. I had to call around a good bit before I found out but here it is. Walden Engineers out of Asheville did the actual work. They were hired by Resorts International."

Stephen went on while my mind remained empty.

"Say, was your dad getting ready to sell? I'm not supposed to say this because of being involved with the Chamber of Commerce but I sure hate to see another tract of mountain land fall into the hands of a big developer like that."

"Stephen, how do I get in touch with this... company?"

"Easy. Just call Carl Owen at their branch office in Athens. He should be able to clear up this whole thing for you."

I thanked him while in the distance his voice said something about us getting together for lunch or dinner soon. I gave no definite answer.

"I'll get back with him," I thought. "When I've sorted this all out."

I dialed the number given me by directory assistance for Resorts International as soon as I hung up from speaking with Stephen. There was no answer. It was after five so I would have to wait until morning. I fidgeted about, at loose ends, and then decided to go shopping for food. I'd cook my nervousness away with a dinner that would please even Isaac, and invite him to join me. Then he could see first hand that I didn't eat rabbit food and coffee all the time.

I drove to Millers General Store where my parents had bought everything smaller than a pick-up truck since they were both children. Anything was available there from thread to bailed hay to canned soup and work shoes, and the building also included the Laurel Hill Post Office.

Immediately upon entering the front door I sensed that Hank Miller no longer ran the place. A row of cracker barrels stood in front of the counter, likely because that was someone's image of what a country store should have.

The pot bellied stove was clean and polished and showed no sign of ever having had a fire in it. An obviously new checkerboard sat on a table between two chairs. The aura of authenticity was gone. A young man with a fake looking mustache and bib apron stood behind the counter.

"May I help you?" The accent was definitely not Laurel Hill.

"I'll look around for a few minutes," I said.

"Let us know if we can help you find anything. And if you'd like to know the history of the place there's a free brochure over in front of the post office."

I fought an urge to very politely inform him that I, my parents, grandparents and their parents, plus all the natives of Laurel Hill were a part of that history. We had lived what he called history.

I hurriedly finished gathering my groceries and paid for them, never letting him know that I wasn't just another tourist. After all, he was only a small part of what I was beginning to realize was a great conglomeration of effort to turn this mountain community into a wall-to-wall resort.

After situating my grocery bags in the trunk of my rental car and slamming the lid, I reached for the door handle, preoccupied with some vague recollection about the store, when a voice full of energetic enthusiasm shrieked in recognition.

"Rachel! Rachel Myers! What are you doing here? I thought you were in Arizona!"

I whirled to face a vision of wildly swinging blond hair and flashing blue eyes.

"Donna Matheson! I thought you were in Miami!"

We hugged each other with every bit as much enthusiasm as when we were sixteen and Donna would show up in Monday morning homeroom with the class ring of her latest conquest. We ended up at my house, hugging coffee cups, catching up, and reminiscing. She hadn't heard about Dad, either. She had just gotten into town that morning.

"I'm so sorry, Rachel. Your dad was always so cool."

Fighting the sadness that threatened to dampen our reunion, I told her briefly about Dad's blindness but very little about the circumstances surrounding his death.

"But, I want to hear about you," I said. "How long will you be here?"

"Oh," the Donna I remembered answered nonchalantly, "from now on, I suppose. I've taken a position as convention coordinator with one of the biggies here, Elk Mountain Resort."

"How could you leave a super job with an airline to come here to work? The pay can't be as good…"

Donna interrupted with wildly gesturing hands.

"But, it is! Even better, in fact. And I'll have benefits and a lot of privileges free of charge that I have to pay for now. Skiing and indoor tennis in the winter, and golf of course, and practically anything going on in the summer. It's a great job, and besides, I've had a secret yen to come back home for a while anyway."

That was a shock. That was definitely unlike the old Donna who used to hold her head and groan about the bleakness of mountain life and her totally boring family.

"Well, I suppose the area has changed more than I thought. But, indoor tennis? When I've been here for visits over the years, I never took the time to drive around and I suppose I really didn't pay much attention to Dad and Isaac talking about changes."

Donna filled me in on the history of the past few years and how the tourist industry had boomed, even when the economy was dragging elsewhere in the country.

"These businesses around here are definitely not catering to the oil on velvet trade," she explained. "They're after people who can afford to lay out two thousand dollars for a short weekend. Or, buy a second or third home for upwards of five hundred thousand. That's why they can afford me. They've just now cast their eye on developing a big convention center. They know I'll be good at that – so many connections."

"You'll have a real juggling act," I said, "between the local people and the newcomers."

"I know and I can't say it doesn't bother me, like it does a lot of people, the attitude of some of those who come here from other places. And you can always tell - when they pronounce Appalachia Appa*lay*chia you know they're from off the mountain and that they're eaten up with that condescending attitude. Yes, I know what some of them think of mountain people. They speak pretty freely in front of me because they think I'm not from around here.

"A friend of mine, Carrie Harmon and her husband, moved back here after living away for nearly twenty years. They opened an arts and crafts shop. Because she'd lost her mountain accent, a lot of her customers assumed she was from off the mountain. After learning that Carrie and Dave were year-round residents, a woman leaned close one day and whispered to Carrie, *'How do you deal with the locals?'*

"Carrie swears that you could have substituted lepers for locals based on the woman's tone of voice. But I digress, as usual. What I do is beat them at their own game. My salary will be double what they could get some transplant for, because, as I said, I've got the connections!"

Donna had to leave but promised to call with a time when we could get together for a real catch-up talk. A sudden thought came to me.

"Donna, let me ask you, did you ever know Ed McKinney?"

" What an odd question! No, I never knew him any better than anyone else did. He was older than us and not married when he came here to work at the bank.

"To tell you the truth, I don't ever remember seeing him with anyone. But, I do know this; I can remember sometimes seeing him standing around when we came out of the theater. Always gave me a creepy feeling like he was watching us. What's your interest in Ed McKinney?"

My response was not very forthcoming because I knew how difficult it would be to explain the situation to her since I could not yet explain it to myself. She reacted in her usual laid-back way and did not press me for details.

"Well, got to run. And, about your dad, if there's anything I can do, let me know, okay? And say hi to Spud when you see him."

I had not kept in as close contact with Stephen as with Donna. I knew he had gotten a master's degree in engineering in Raleigh and had married shortly thereafter. I had heard from Donna, who attended all high school class reunions within four years up or down of ours, that Stephen's wife had died in a car crash when they had been married only five years.

I didn't know if he'd remarried, although I couldn't imagine that he hadn't. He was by nature a settled person, reasonable, quiet and calm. But, capable of sudden bursts of enthusiasm. I recalled one such incident that dwelt permanently in my memory.

In the autumn of the twelfth grade, Spud showed up at my house with everything we'd need to go for a picnic and horseback ride. Picnic lunch packed in our saddlebags, we rode, climbing up and down and over mountains until we were far beyond the borders of my father's property. Only when an unusual rock formation came into view did I realize where we were. The Pinnacles were several gigantic rocks that faced in different directions. Girlish goose bumps crept along my spine. There were always rumors of black bears and mountain lions being seen there. And timber rattlers.

I enjoyed a shiver of anticipation for the romance of possible danger. Stephen had found a trail that led to a small clearing on the west side of the rocks where we unsaddled and spread our picnic on the ground. After lunch we used our saddles, cowboy fashion, for pillows. The horses were content after the long climb, to stand quietly and nibble at leaves.

We turned to each other but after a few awkward kisses and a bit of fumbling we decided that kind of relationship was just not for us. We were too much like brother and sister. We stayed the best of friends after mutually agreeing that Donna was never to know of our failed attempt at romance. She would have tormented us about it for the rest of our lives.

Chapter Nine

Hammered and breaded pork loin sizzled in an iron skillet while small whole potatoes danced in boiling water. A pan of cornbread sat ready for the oven. A slice of seasoning ham I had put into the green beans was beginning to fill the kitchen with a long forgotten aroma. I shredded cabbage for coleslaw and was adding chopped onions and grated carrots when Isaac arrived.

"Smells like it did when your mama was alive," he said wistfully.

"Come on and sit down," I said. "It's almost done. And I want you to watch me eat so you can stop worrying about me starving!"

Halfway through the meal he looked up.

"You heard from Stephen yet?"

"I did. And, about more than just the markers. That whole section of property has been surveyed. By Resorts International, no less! Stephen says they have a branch office in Athens and I intend to be sitting by the door when Mr. Carl Owen comes in to work in the morning!"

Isaac was trying to control his anger. I could tell by the way the veins in his neck stood out and how the little depression fluttered below his Adam's apple. He exploded.

"Why the hell do these damned people from everywhere in the world come to the mountains and try to take over? They ain't got no stopping place. Just buy or half steal or scare people into selling their land. They're way worse than the land speculators back during the depression. Rachel, sometimes I don't see any hope for anybody living here except the damned tourists. You can't go off squirrel huntin' in the woods anymore for fear you'll hit one of their houses.

" And that's not even the worst of it. At least them that's got money build nice houses and lay out a road around the trees and rocks. But the ones that can't afford a nice place, why, they've gone to digging out a hole in the side of a mountain that's way too steep to use for anything else. Then, they'll stick one of them trailers back in the hole.

"Before God, I think that's the ugliest sight I've ever seen. All that bare dirt and rock cut down so deep there's no chance of anything ever growing on it. Reminds me of the landslides back during the forty flood."

Isaac's mention of bare land reminded me of the steep bare mountainsides I had seen from the top of Pigeon Crest.

He shook his head and grimaced.

"Yeah, its them Christmas tree growers. Why is it, Rachel, that some folks just don't know when to slow down or stop? You know they've been growing Christmas trees here for thirty years or more. But in the beginning they were planted on land that wouldn't grow much else. Then all of the land that use to grow cabbage and beans was planted. After that, the only way to go was up so now they're scraping off the mountainsides and planting them there."

Isaac drank from his coffee mug and reached for another piece of cornbread.

"Don't get me wrong. I don't have a problem with the tree farming. It puts honest income into many a man's pocket. It's just that they're so almighty shortsighted. One of these years we're going to have a long rainy season like the one that caused the forty flood I just mentioned. Them mountainsides are going to break loose and slide, and no amount of so-called erosion control is going to stop it."

He ate silently for a while and then spoke again.

"You know Paul fixed up my pay in a trust a long time ago and I get my check regular as clockwork? Well, I've been working around for other people, mostly to fill in time that wasn't needed here anymore. I help a friend in his auction business sometimes, just odds and ends kind of work. And I've lent a hand to a few other fellers now and then. But I just won't do any work in Christmas trees.

"Course, hardly anybody works in them now except for the Mexicans. And that's another thing that gets my goat. You've got these people, most of them not able to speak or read English, and they're turned loose with deadly chemicals to spray two hundred acres of Christmas trees.

"How often do you reckon they use twice as much as they're supposed to? And where does it go with the first rain? Into the branches and streams and rivers! And, at the same time you've got the eco-nuts worrying about some poor farmer's cow pasture being too close to a creek that feeds into the New River."

Isaac shook his head as his voice slowly wound down. I knew his frustration and mine did not stem only from tourism or Christmas trees, but was due to an assortment of events beginning before my father's death and ending with the knowledge, for Isaac, at least, that the very mountain he "laid eyes to every morning" was in the first stages of becoming an alien land.

I promised myself at that moment that never while I was alive and had control over it would even a square inch of the land I had grown up on be sold.

We calmed down and changed the subject. Isaac complimented me on the supper.

"Except for the corn bread," he teased. "Don't you know you're supposed to put in enough baking soda to make it yellow?"

I shushed him and did not let on that I had baked it from self-rising mix, a deed that no true mountain cook would own up to.

"Let me know what you find out from that Owen yahoo," Isaac called back from the kitchen door. "You know I'll be glad to go with you if you want me to."

I declined his offer but said I'd come by to see him as soon as I had talked to Owen. I tried to watch television that night but since Dad didn't have a satellite system my choices were slim. Mingled with the images on the screen were the images of the events of the last few days. I could not concentrate on either and went to bed, hopeful for a restful night.

Through my open window, just before I fell asleep, I heard what my father had called a 'rain crow' because they were nearly always heard before a summer rain. I had been glancing through a book on birds once and found that it was actually a yellow-billed Cuckoo, a bird so elusive that few people can boast of ever having seen it.

I dreamed of David again but pleasantly this time. No discernible story, just his face smiling at me in the Arizona sun. I half woke and promised myself I'd call him in the morning. No more e-mails.

However, the next morning David was far in the back of my mind behind Resorts International and Carl Owen. I forced myself to eat a bowl of cereal and dressed carefully.

I looked at my reflection in the mirror, comfortable with my appearance. No longer school girlish, but a woman, mature, and as Isaac would put it, "With a little extra space between the eyes!"

Athens had grown to the point that there was no way to tell where the old parts ended and the new began. Many buildings had a pseudo Swiss Chalet look. Somehow I doubted that there was much similarity to real Swiss style.

Resorts International was typical of the other new buildings in its style, just more flashy. I stood in the slickly paved and landscaped parking lot trying to get a sense of what had once been in that spot.

Across the street behind me was the new courthouse, a brick cracker box that had replaced a beautiful Greco-Roman structure built before the turn of the twentieth century. Then, with sinking heart, I remembered. The space had held the old Smithey's Department Store and its graveled parking lot where farmers had come to set up and sell their produce.

The highlight of a trip to Athens on a Saturday in the summer when I was a little girl was an old man who sold watermelons right off the back of his dilapidated pick-up truck. He had a cooler rigged up to his truck battery and the melons were icy cold. He would sell you a whole, a half, or a single slice to eat right then.

Dad always bought a whole one to take home and a slice for each of us. I could remember the color, the chill, the sweetness and that it was impossible to keep the sticky juice from running down my chin.

"Well," I thought. "Another one bites the dust."

An attractive young receptionist sat behind a small ineffectual desk. High on a wall was a large logo that incorporated the letters RIC.

"May I give him your name, please," she chirped when I asked to see Carl Owen.

"It wouldn't matter," I said, "he wouldn't know me. But, it's Rachel Myers."

After a half-guarded few words into the phone, she showed me through a very tall door. The man pouring himself a cup of coffee could have been an executive in any large business anywhere.

Pinstriped suit, white shirt, blue tie. Slim with brown hair beginning to thin on top. He smiled pleasantly, but I could sense an air of coolness. He moved toward me, offering his hand. I took it for a brief shake.

"Ms. Myers? Carl Owen. Will you have coffee?"

"Thank you, no," I answered hurriedly and plunged right in. "I need to know about some unauthorized surveying that your company had done on my father's property."

His head gave a surprised little jerk as he looked up from his coffee.

"Ah, Ms. Myers. You're the daughter, then."

"Yes, I'm the daughter." I could feel the sarcasm on my tongue. "Paul Myers was my father. You might have heard that he died last week?"

His face registered no surprise. He simply murmured, "Sorry to hear that, Ms. Myers."

My voice almost broke when I spoke again.

"Would you please explain?"

He seemed at a loss for words for a few moments. He moved straight forward in his chair and clasped his hands together on the desktop.

"Well, that's a prime piece of property there, Ms. Myers. And when we found out that there was a possibility that it might come on the market sometime soon, of course, we were interested. That's our business, after all, development."

"Mr. Owen." I strained to keep my voice normal and to retain my patience. "I'm not interested at all in your company's business. I want to know what the hell made you think you had the right to send a surveying crew on my father's property to see if it was suitable for a ski slope?"

His eyes widened in obvious surprise that I knew what the markers represented. He paused before he spoke again. He watched me closely as he took a file from his side drawer and opened it on his desk.

"We have here an authorization signed by one Ed McKinney, who is listed as a broker for your father."

There was smugness to his voice that infuriated me but I was determined to keep my cool. It was all beginning to come together. I bit my lip until the pain cleared my head.

"Please explain the word 'broker' as you're using it."

"Like real estate broker or agent, Ms. Myers. I understand that Mr. McKinney dabbles in real estate in addition to banking."

I waged a new battle to stay in control of my wits. I must get all the information that I could out of Carl Owen before going to see McKinney.

"Did you ever speak directly to my father about this?"

"Why, no. There was no reason to. We deal with brokers all the time. Sometimes never even meet the actual owner."

I stood up on shaky knees. But there was nothing shaky about my voice.

"Mr. Owen, I have a feeling in the very near future, Paul Myers is one owner that you're going to regret not meeting!"

"Now look here!" he responded. "We've done nothing unethical or illegal, not in the slightest. And the property still belongs to you, doesn't it?"

I started to leave and then turned back.

"I suppose you're going to tell me that you didn't know about the lien that the bank, where incidentally, McKinney works, has on my property?"

There, I had said it. "My property!" And it was. And I realized at that moment that I was willing to do whatever I must to keep it. I went on before he could answer.

"Oh, Mr. Owen, don't ever play word games! What you think shows too plainly on your face!"

"Look," he countered, a slight frown beginning to crease his brow. "I don't want any trouble. I'll level with you and then you and Ed McKinney work it out between you. I had nothing to do with that loan. In fact, I didn't know anything about it until after McKinney contacted me about what he thought was a prime piece of property for a ski slope.

"After we surveyed the land, and I agree that was a little underhanded, maybe a little unethical, but certainly not illegal, we realized that it was more than suitable and then he told me about the lien on the property. Said it would be considered in default in a few months and he knew the old man, er...your father, couldn't pay it off.

"He seemed to know all the details so I asked him jokingly if he had made the loan himself. He very matter-of-factly said, of course, and that he had made sure that the old man spent every penny of it on something that wouldn't turn a profit. McKinney was to get title to the property when the bank foreclosed and we agreed to pay him seven hundred and fifty thousand for the deed."

Through all of this I stayed calm, at least outwardly. I was only hearing what I had half-suspected before, except the price. Inconceivable!

"I'm not condoning anything questionable the man might have done, either legally or morally. But, we're a development company and if we started questioning every detail in the background of every deal we make, we'd soon be out of business."

I had forgotten I was standing. I watched the hint of smugness that came over Carl Owens's face with his last words. My knees trembled.

"Did McKinney ever mention me in connection with paying off the loan? How could he be sure that I couldn't pay it off?"

"I'm not certain of that. But he indicated that Myers didn't have anyone in any financial position to be making a payoff of that amount. Said he had him in the palm of his hand, something about taking care of all his business for him.

"It was a bit jumbled and I never did really understand what he was getting at, and quite frankly, didn't want to."

In my most polite voice, I said, "Mr. Owen, you've been most helpful. I thank you."

His face began to beam at my words, but lost its glow as I continued.

"But, let me tell you something. This time it might have benefited your *business* if you'd asked a few more questions.

"Just what do you think will happen when Resorts International and Mr. Carl Owen are implicated along with Ed McKinney in a murder investigation?"

I stood for a moment to let my words sink in and to see his reaction. His face had turned ashen and he did not speak. I turned and walked out.

It felt good to hear that door slam behind me. I did not look at the receptionist but heard her say "What?" in response to the loud echoing bang.

I sat in my car in the parking lot counting the large drops of rain that had spattered the windshield. For the first time since I arrived in Laurel Hill I was at a loss as to what came next. I wanted to see Ed McKinney more than anything else.

But I was honest enough with myself to admit that he would come out ahead in any confrontation we might have at this point. Where my emotions were involved, I was always at a disadvantage.

The rain began in earnest now, no longer a sprinkle but a full-fledged autumn shower. By the time I reached home, clouds were darkening the mountaintops and fingers of lightening had begun to shoot up behind Rocky Face.

Chapter Ten

Isaac awaited me at the kitchen table. He seemed to have aged just since the previous night. I believe he had anticipated what I would find out from Carl Owen because his face showed neither the surprise nor anger that I feared. He seemed almost complacent.

For a moment, I was glad, then from somewhere long ago, a half-forgotten phrase went through my head, *...have to watch out for Isaac when he gets quiet, not when he's making a lot of noise.*

Some chemistry, possibly from our mutual closeness to each other and to my father, made me aware, like moving pictures on a screen, of just what was going through his mind. He rose stiffly from his chair and I grabbed his arm.

"No, Isaac, no! In the first place, if Ed McKinney did what we think he did, do you suppose he'd hesitate to kill again if he's threatened? And then, who would I have left if something happened to you?"

He stood ramrod stiff with my fingers still gripping his arm.

"Look, he's not going to win, Isaac. He's not getting the land. I have the money to take care of the loan. And we'll make him pay. If we can prove he hid Dad's pills, we'll see him prosecuted for it."

I was exhausted, drained from my confrontation with Owen and now this. I played my final card when Isaac broke free and headed for the door.

"Dad wouldn't want you to do this, Isaac. He wouldn't want you to take a chance on leaving me completely alone!"

He stumbled back to the table and slumped into a chair. Dry sobs racked his shoulders. I had seen a man cry before, like Dad at Mom's funeral, but never anyone in the throes of such heartache and helpless anger.

After a while his shoulders stopped heaving and he raised his head and took out his handkerchief. He wiped his eyes and blew his nose, then spoke in a deadly quiet voice.

"He will pay, Rachel. I'll try it your way first, but if that don't work, I'll take care of him in my own way."

His quiet declaration spread a chill over me. I knew I wouldn't have long to go about the job myself. Isaac left, saying he had work to do. I followed him to the door.

"Now, remember, you promised…"

"I told you, girl. I won't do anything until you've tried it your way. That was a promise and I'll keep it. Just don't let it take too long."

I reached for the phone, unsure of whom to call first, David or Wade Gwynn. Instead, it rang. I recognized the voice in spite of the static from the thunderstorm.

"Mrs. Campbell, Lydia, how wonderful to hear from you!"

Her voice came and went on the bad connection but I understood enough to realize that she had just learned of Dad's death.

"Rachel, I feel so awful. The couple I work for and I just got back from a cruise. Mrs. Marshall's health is pretty bad and I just got around to opening a week's worth of mail this morning."

She began to cry. I tried to console her but it was difficult with so much static on the line.

"Mrs. Campbell, there's something going on here that I can't go into right now, but I might want you to come back and testify abut Dad's relationship with Ed McKinney."

"You just let me know when! Nothing would keep me from telling what he's like. He's the devil incarnate!"

With that, the noise stopped and our connection was severed. I would call her again when I needed her.

I picked up my cell phone and hit the direct dial for David's office, then hung up quickly. I was in no state to carry on a long conversation with him about us, even though I knew what my answer was going to be. I didn't know exactly when it became definite, never consciously knew when I made the decision. But I had made it.

Yes, I wanted to marry him. Yes, I wanted to take the chance. I hoped we could make it but even if we didn't, at least I would have given it a true effort, I would have worked at it. Maybe that was the secret, that success was not guaranteed but the honest effort given could sustain one even with failure. Still, I was not prepared to talk to David, not with all this other swarming in my head. I went to my laptop and sent an e-mail instead.

"Transfer two hundred and thirty thousand dollars ($230,000.00)..." After the necessary information, I added, "No questions now – do you still want to marry me?"

That behind me, I dialed Wade Gwynn's number. His secretary said Wade was in Raleigh on business but would be back in his office by nine the next morning. I cursed under my breath. I had hoped to get his advice right away so we could go to the sheriff that afternoon. I didn't want to go alone.

Even in these liberated days, some people could be awfully unconcerned with a woman who took on too much without a man at her side. So, I would wait until tomorrow. But it would be an agonizing wait, not knowing whether Isaac's patience would erode or whether Carl Owen would tip off Ed McKinney that I was on to him. I knew I stood a strong chance of never being able to prove that McKinney had committed a crime. Manipulation was not against the law.

How he must have worked on my father's emotions, convincing him that his only child had refused to help when everything he owned was at stake. That thought was painful.

If McKinney was punished only for that it would have to be severe to even begin to make up for being reminded for the rest of my life that my father died thinking that I had refused to help him.

The thunderstorm quieted down and the rain had leveled off to a steady mist by early afternoon. Isaac came back to the house and I could see that he had been working around the barn. He glanced down guiltily when he saw me look at his shoes.

"Oh, come on, Isaac! Don't worry about that. There's hot coffee if you want some and an apple pie I bought at Miller's yesterday."

He pulled out a chair after refusing my offer of pie and coffee.

"You're going to make somebody a good wife one day, Rachel. No man likes to have to take off his shoes before he can come into his own house."

I told Isaac about David then. I had barely mentioned him before but now it poured out like a flood. His personality so suited to mine. Just this way enough to offset that way of mine. His sense for business, his kindness and generous spirit.

"Doesn't he have any faults at all?" Isaac teased.

"Yes, of course, but they are so far overshadowed by the rest of him that they just don't matter. He works at being what he is, Isaac. He just doesn't happen to be that way. And he lets me be myself, too. He doesn't try to pattern me after his mother or his sister or his first girlfriend. He…"

Again Isaac teased, "Sounds like Superman to me!"

I was happy to see him in a better mood. I told him we would go to Wade Gwynn's office in the morning and find out the best way to approach the sheriff about the situation.

His eyes clouded a bit but he remained calm. I searched for something to fill the afternoon. The sun had come out, it was only three o'clock and I did not want to spend the rest of the day brooding.

"I know, Isaac, let's drive to Athens and eat a sandwich and then come back by Worley and stop at the old school. It's still there, isn't?"

"All right," he grumbled. "Long as we get back by six thirty. I promised Jack Whaley I'd go to another of them Soil Conservation meetings with him. He's just like an old woman. Can't go nowhere or do nothing without somebody right by his side!"

Athens had more restaurants than any town of its size in western North Carolina, so boasted the Athens Daily. I believed it too after Isaac and I had driven around town for a few minutes. And like doctors, they were mostly specialists. Italian, Japanese, Mexican, Seafood, Burgers, Steaks or Chicken.

Finally we came to a bright red train caboose, of all things, that had been converted to a small deli sandwich shop. It was exactly the kind of place I had been hoping for. I had a hot Reuben sandwich and Isaac had plain ham on rye bread. My sandwich was good but would have been better with a cold beer.

But Sheppard County was dry, no brown bagging or liquor store, just beer and wine at the food markets and not even that on Sundays because of their Blue Law, one of only a few that still existed in North Carolina. That was one area where the newcomers had failed to have their way.

Isaac was quiet and seemed to get more so as time passed. I could tell he was thinking. When he didn't offer to pay for our meals as we left, I knew he was concentrating awfully hard on something.

In the car I asked, "What's on your mind, Isaac? Anything new?"

"No," he answered. "I just can't help thinking about Paul. There's got to be some kind of justice. Not much good just talking about it though."

Thankfully, we had reached the school. It sat in a small valley just off the highway. Built by the WPA in the nineteen thirties, it stood like a monument instead of a building. The outer walls were native stone and the architectural style had been described as eclectic, with elements of several architectural styles. A little bit Gothic, some Federal and even some Tudor elements worked together to form a building that would have fitted very well on any large college campus.

The structure hadn't been used for a school in over twenty years. There was a new brick building that housed grades one through six just outside of Athens. A new consolidated middle and high school took care of grades seven through twelve.

Isaac had told me that many of the children in the county boarded buses before seven in the morning to reach their school by eight o'clock. But this school building sat here, rock-hard and commanding respect.

The Sheppard Historical Society had used it for years as a museum of sorts. Their space was small but at least all the exhibits pertained to the area and had historical significance. Displayed along with items concerning school and mountain farms and famous floods was horse and buggy doctor Jim Lowe's medical bag that he had carried for nearly sixty years.

I could remember my mother talking about Dr. Lowe. She recalled a time when her mother was a child during an epidemic of diphtheria. Dr. Lowe went from house to house around the mountains for twelve straight weeks. He'd fall asleep from exhaustion but his horse knew the way so well that he'd go on and stop at the next house on his route. My grandmother had died from a weak heart that was the result of having diphtheria during that epidemic.

I was conjuring up things I didn't want to dwell on. I wanted to remember school days, and school friends and times when life was simple. Like the last day of the eighth grade.

We all knew the school was closing and that we would return to a spanking new building near Athens. That knowledge made us more than a little sad, the idea that we were the last eighth grade to ever graduate from this building where most of our parents had gone to school. I could almost hear voices, Mrs. Horton's singsong, "Rachel Myers, Stephen Phillips? Where are you? We've still got to hand out the perfect attendance certificates!"

Another voice, this one Stephen, low and sad, "Rachel, just think, we ain't never going to come here to school another day."

And mine in return, "Don't say ain't, Spud. And so what, it's just an old building anyway."

Then, a sob caught in my throat. Finally there was the kiss, the one Stephen reminded me of earlier. As small as the flutter of moth wings on the side of my cheek, I grant you, but a kiss nonetheless.

Isaac had disappeared behind the building. I passed under the low limbs of an oak tree that we used to climb in second grade. We preferred it to the monkey bars but had been forced to stop our climbing because of insurance concerns.

"Here," Isaac said, holding out his hand.

It was a large green striped agate, a 'log roller' as my father had called them. I rolled the marble around on my palm and wondered if today's children would even know how to play with them. They had probably gone the way of Jacks in this world of Game Boys and X-Boxes.

I supposed it could have been dropped recently but believing it had been lost by some long ago student, maybe even my father, and had just now worked its way back up to daylight was much more pleasant and suited my nostalgic frame of mind.

Isaac was looking at his watch. I headed for the car, not wanting to make him late for his friend. I figured the busier he stayed, the less time he would have to think about Ed McKinney. Now, how was I going to keep myself from dwelling on him?

We went by the post office on our way home and found a large manilla envelope from Flagstaff full of my father's letters. I showed them to Isaac one after the other. They went back for several years and there was not a single sentence that could be construed as a plea for help.

After a supper of leftovers from last night's dinner, and the last of the bottle of wine I had found, I made a list of things to talk over with Wade Gwynn. I didn't want to forget anything, no matter how seemingly insignificant. I laid my information out carefully. Every item was important and to be considered soberly if I was to make the right decision.

Pursuing this course I had set myself, meant stepping into unknown waters; not pursuing it meant continued frustration at never knowing the whole truth. I wanted justice done, of course, but I also felt the heat of a tiny flame that demanded vengeance for my father's death.

As the wine warmed me, Ed McKinney and my father's death became all mixed up with Isaac's talk about the down side of tourism and how it was affecting the area.

That night I finally went to sleep with Carl Owen's words echoing in my head. "We're in the development business and if we asked questions…"

I dreamed that an enormous machine driven by Carl Owen had been set up on Pigeon Crest. A great metal ball swung back and forth.. I was on the edge of the cliff and every time the machine would turn to face me, Owen would say over and over like a broken record, "The development business, Ms. Myers, the development business, Ms. Myers…"

Then came Stephen, his face faded like it was in the newspaper clipping and with him were Wade Gwynn and Isaac. They could not stop the swinging ball either but when David appeared the ball changed to a rusty metal bucket and made clanking noises as it bounced off the rock.

Thunder half awakened me but then I went back to sleep, comfortable in the knowledge that it was just a dream and the rock and the farm and I were safe with David.

Chapter Eleven

The morning dawned auspiciously enough. There had been a light rain during the night. The trees and grass sparkled as sun rose in a cloudless sky, sending its first faint pink glow across the mountaintops. The closer hills and valleys took shape, emerging distinct once again from the formless night.

Even before the rim of the sun had shown itself above the eastern forest, I was wide-awake and pondering the events that whirled in my head.

With list in hand and Isaac by my side, we entered Wade Gwynn's office with an air of purpose. He offered us coffee and settled back, hands clasped behind his head to listen.

Of course, he already knew about the loan and the surveying but that was all. His eyebrows shot up when I read off the other things on my list, especially my conversation with Carl Owen, but by the time I had finished, his attitude was one of caution.

"Well," he began, "lets look at the facts we've got here as objectively as we can. Here's a man, let's try for a minute to forget that he's your father, all right? A blind man, who nearly two years ago is befriended by a younger man, someone he has known for some time but never been close to. The younger man spends a lot of time with the blind man, even begins to take care of his business and correspondence, runs off his faithful housekeeper, tries his best to keep other people away.

"We know it's a verifiable fact McKinney organized the bank loan, that he signed the papers as the agent to give permission for the surveying to be done. We know what the money from the loan was spent for. We know that two sizable checks have not been cashed and are missing. We know the bottle of pills was hidden and we have Doctor Hartley's statement that Paul might have lived if he'd had his pills.

"But, with all of that, we don't have a single item that could be used against Ed McKinney in a court of law. The only thing that would be of use would have been your father's testimony that McKinney had coerced him."

Isaac was red-faced and looked as if he might explode at any moment. I tried to keep my wits about me but finally gave in.

"So, what you're telling me is that through all of this Ed McKinney has operated within the law, that he has not committed a single illegal act, nothing that we can bring charges against him for?"

Wade nodded. "We can go to the district attorney if you want to but I don't think he'll advise you any differently than I have. See, if McKinney had signed and cashed those checks or personally spent any of the money from the loan or already profited in any way from your father's actions, we'd have something to go on.

"Even his presence in the house the night Paul died can't be used. It's a fact that Paul died from a heart attack and there's no way for us to ever prove that McKinney moved that bottle of pills."

Pain and anger welled within me, churning like food in an overfull stomach. Isaac maintained a deadly silence.

"Rachel," Wade went on. "I believe what you believe. I know in my heart and soul that Ed McKinney did everything that you're accusing him of. I know he manipulated your father, made him suspicious, confused him, all of that.

"But there's not one iota of proof to substantiate it. And proof is the only thing that counts in a court of law!"

The silence became almost deafening. Blood pulsed in my ears and I could hear each beat of my heart. I could no longer make sense of my thoughts. It was like a terrible nightmare in the middle of the day; faces, voices, feelings, swirling in and out and around, out of control. The only thing that remained steadfast and clear was the name Ed McKinney, Ed McKinney, Ed McKinney.

Wade tried to console me, taking my hand and patting my shoulder. His attempt to comfort me affected me strangely and I struggled to stand. My legs were weak and trembled as if I had walked a great distance. Suddenly, the floor came up to meet me.

"Rachel! Rachel!" Wade's voice seemed to come from far away.

I wondered why he had just stopped talking like that in the middle of the sentence. He was usually so precise, always finishing what he began.

Then I opened my eyes and he was on his knees over me holding a paper cup. An arm cradled my head and I saw Isaac's worried face upside down behind me. I struggled to sit up. Wade insisted I drink some water, so I did.

"My God, I don't believe this! I haven't fainted since high school when Old Miss Batten made us dissect a live frog in biology!"

I was genuinely embarrassed at my reaction to the reality that we were helpless as far as prosecuting Ed McKinney. What was left to do?

Suddenly I felt very tired and almost wished that I had never found out anything about anything. Of course, except the loan. I could have paid that off and just always wondered why Dad had borrowed that much money…no, that was impossible. I could no more have ignored all the questions about my father than I could have ignored the hidden bottle of pills.

My heart ached and a black anger simmered within me. Could I ever accept the actuality that Ed McKinney would go unpunished for the hand he had in wrecking my father's life? Maybe it would grow on me, maybe each day that passed would wear away a little more of the anger and bitterness.

But I knew I would never get over it completely, never entirely forget. I would always harbor a desire for McKinney to be punished.

My thoughts reminded me of Isaac, who stood waiting for me by the door. His face was calm, his blue eyes bright but without the anger I expected in them. He shook his head in answer to the question he saw in my eyes, as if to say, "No, I'm not going to do anything foolish. Not now, anyway."

Again the mental exchange between us startled me. It was almost as if the words had been spoken aloud. Wade was vying for my attention.

"Rachel, let Ethel and me take you out to dinner this evening. We could talk this over in more detail and who knows, we might come up with some solution."

I had opened my mouth to answer when Stephen Phillips stuck his head in the door and interrupted.

"No way, Wade! I've got first dibs on her this evening. Right, Rachel?"

The idea of an evening with Spud was by far more appealing than one with Wade and Ethel. If my memory served me correctly Ethel's brand of conversation consisted entirely of clothes, places to eat, and her Pekinese dog named "Moochy." I turned to Wade.

"Well, I actually did promise Stephen…"

"All right," Wade answered, not too unwillingly. "But, lets get together soon. We really might come up with something."

"I'll pick you up at six," Stephen said. "There's a little place over in Athens that has a great menu."

I told Stephen I'd be ready at six and Isaac and I drove home. I was beginning to get accustomed to this feeling of defeat. Up, down, think you've got it all figured out one minute and you're back to square one in the next.

Even though the hour was early, I was exhausted and I suppose it showed. Isaac told me I'd better pack it in for a while. After he left, I latched the kitchen door and ran a bath.

I lay in the hot water and tried to dissolve as much of the day from my consciousness as possible. After I got out of the tub I decided to lie down on top of the bed covers for a while. Instead, I climbed between the sheets.

The next thing I was aware of was the sound of an unfamiliar ringing. It wasn't a telephone. Finally I realize it was the seldom-used front door bell. I hastily wrapped myself in a long bathrobe and scooted downstairs. Isaac's forehead was pressed against the door glass.

"You latched the screen door in the kitchen and I couldn't get in. Thought I'd better wake you in time for you to get ready by six."

All at once I was aware that the sun was low and the day was growing dusky.

"My God, I must have died! What time is it, Isaac?"

He consulted his ancient pocket watch. "Ten of five."

I rushed to get ready and Isaac saw me to the door when Stephen arrived.

"I'll lock up before I leave," he called after me.

The drive to Athens was pleasant. Since I didn't have to drive, I could observe more clearly the extent of the 'tourist' invasion, as Isaac had put it. Real estate and construction businesses were everywhere. And to go along with these, there were two new building supply stores. Interior design and decorative arts were obviously popular businesses with newcomers because I counted several along the way.

All along the twelve-mile road to Athens were entrances to new developments. A few appeared modest but most of them were flanked by expensive gates through which was visible curb and gutter streets, probably better than any public street or road in the county. I started reading the names: Eden Woods, Pine Village, Quail Hollow, Fox Run and Hunter's Rest.

We passed golf courses, at least three of them between the towns of Laurel Hill and Athens. Rearranging mountains one truckload at a time had provided more level land than most mountain farmers had ever seen.

Lakes were obviously popular also. I spotted one that completely covered land on which an old man had lived when I was a girl. Dad and Isaac had taken me with them once when they went to bargain for a rabbit beagle.

"Where in the world is all this money coming from?" I asked Stephen.

"Right where you just said, the world. There are property owners in this county from almost any state you can name and a lot from other countries. I was out in Feldon Acres the other day and I met two men on a couple of good-looking horses. I spoke to one of them and he nodded and then turned to his interpreter to answer me.

"He was from Saudi Arabia and was visiting his twenty-one-room vacation house he had just built near the Blue Ridge Parkway. According to the interpreter, that was the latest addition to a long list of houses he owns all over the world."

The thought of that much wealth in a place like Laurel Hill left me speechless. And I had thought the lien on Dad's property was a lot of money. Stephen continued.

"You know, land's going for as much as a hundred and fifty thousand an acre in some parts of the county. Half-acre lots in these already established, so-called 'gated communities' can sell for a hundred thousand."

My education on modern mountain life was certainly moving along!

"But how does that affect the local population, Spud? I mean, the people who were here first. Surely they can't afford…"

"Well, it's a sort of trade-off, I guess. Some people here do have good steady jobs that are the direct result of tourism. Of course, that in itself is a double-edged sword. Most of a good paycheck is eaten up by high property taxes and higher prices on nearly everything, groceries, clothes, gas, than you'll find just off the mountain.

"It's like looking up the hill and seeing a big boulder coming and you can't stop it or get out of its way, so you just stand there and let it roll over you. If a body could just make them see that they are creating the same kind of place they were trying to get away from.

"They're always promoting these *Heritage* festivals and fairs with mythical hillbillies whittling or playing jug music or making moonshine. They've created an image and they won't turn it loose. It would be comical if wasn't so pathetic."

"But, the jobs," I said. "What are they? Do they really pay well?"

"Well, nearly any laborers job you can think of, skilled or unskilled: carpenters, plumbers, electricians, heavy equipment operators, all those pay good wages. And, of course, those jobs are pretty secure as long as the building boom continues. Jobs like maids, waitresses, and store clerks make up the other side of the equation. They pay minimum wage, mostly with no benefits. And they can be fairly undependable, too. If the tourist business is slow, they don't need as many people working.

"There's no denying it's put a lot of money into the county in the way of property taxes. But, at the same time, people who've lived here only a few years and are convinced that their way is always best control a lot of local boards. And some locally owned businesses do benefit, although a lot of them, like Miller's Store, have sold out."

After a moment, Spud went on.

"I suppose it's mainly just getting used to it that's so rough. I hated like hell when they first started coming in with their bulldozers and backhoes and earthmovers. But, I have to say I enjoy some of the advantages. I learned to ski and play golf in college and it's nice not to have to go out of the county for that.

"But, I know what you're getting at. There are not many people born and raised around here that don't dwell on it sooner or later. It's like we've lost our area to some foreign invader who has come in and taken over without us being aware of it until it was too late."

A kind of sad quietness had settled over us by the time we were seated in the restaurant. We made small talk about our surroundings. The food was good but not great and there was no wine list.

"Do you have any plans as far as returning to Arizona?"

The question took me by surprise. I hadn't looked much farther into the future than when I would take care of the loan on the property.

"No, no definite plans yet."

Spud startled me by reaching for my hand and holding it firmly in both of his, giving it a little more than friendly squeeze.

David and I had been an established couple for so long that I had to refresh my memory on how to handle a situation like this without offending or hurting an old and dear friend. And, of course, I chose the wrong way.

"Spud," I quipped. "I didn't know you cared!"

He did look hurt.

"Don't make light of it, Rachel. I think I could let myself grow to care an awful lot for you if I had the chance. You're the first person I've thought that about since I lost Lonnie."

My next thought was "Thank God it hasn't gone too far yet!"

I explained about David and me and the decision I had come to since I had been back in Laurel Hill. I hesitated but felt genuinely obligated to express some interest in his wife. I had only heard that she had died in a car crash but not anything about the circumstances.

Stephen's face went dark, his voice bitter.

"You hear people all the time talk about the dangers of air travel, especially since nine-eleven. Lonnie went with a group on a garden tour of England, stopped off in New York on the way back to spend the weekend with a college friend, then flew to Minnesota to visit her parents and then, from there, flew back to Charlotte.

"All those thousands of miles in the air, then her car is hit by a lousy drunk driver before she got out of the city limits of Charlotte!"

I expressed my sympathy, which was genuine in the light of having just lost my father. We were very quiet for a while. Then Spud spoke in a wry but pleasant tone.

"Well, just let me know if you ever change your mind. I'm sure he won't change his."

I thanked him for his compliment and we went back to our meal, ending it with what the restaurant billed as Apple Delight. I recognized it as only a version of my mother's fried apple pies with a scoop of vanilla ice cream on top.

When we got into the car, I asked Spud if he knew where Ed McKinney lived. At his nod, I said, "Could we drive by there? I promise I'll explain later."

Hickory Gap Road was very crooked so driving was slow. Spud finally stopped at a large mailbox with McKinney, 7019 on the side. The house stood well back from the road and was almost obscured by a row of gigantic hemlocks.

Suddenly, my whole body was seized with a great shiver. At Spud's questioning glance, I said, "Just somebody walking over my grave."

We drove on but that eerie feeling stayed with me until late in the evening.

Chapter Twelve

When sleep finally came, it was a disturbed and restless sleep. I awoke again and again with the feeling that I had had a bad dream but could remember nothing. Sometime in the very early morning, I decided that the restlessness was the result of my long afternoon nap.

That seemed to calm me and I drifted off only to be awakened before daylight by rain beating against the house, lightning flashing through my window, and thunder jarring a loose gutter somewhere close by.

I slept again and when I awoke the clock said nine-thirty. Rain still poured and only a pale weak light filtered through the dark clouds. I lay for another half-hour, just letting my mind skip from one thought to another. I finally settled on a specific one that had come to me the night before when Stephen drove me by Ed McKinney's house.

I still intended to go to see McKinney but not at his house. I would go to the bank instead. After all, the bank was a part of this whole business since they made the loan.

Isaac came by in mid-afternoon but stayed just a little while.

"Something will have to be done about them ditches sooner or later," he said. "Many rains like this and that water'll undermine the highway down there."

On the surface, I understood that there were things around the farm that needed attention but I could not seriously give them any of mine until this McKinney situation was resolved. I hoped it would be soon for I could feel the pressure getting stronger as each day went by.

The afternoon passed but the rain never ceased, just slackened now and then to a heavy drizzle. I tried to read but demands for my attention came at me from all sides.

Finally, I turned on the television. No satellite dish or cable made offerings pretty slight but I finally settled on an old black and white Ingrid Bergman movie called *Gaslight* and stared at the screen until I was sleepy enough to go to bed.

Sunday morning began as beautiful as the previous morning had been ugly. A gorgeous sun bathed everything in gold. The heavy rain had brought down multicolored leaves that lay as if glued to the deck floor and on the walk out front. Not a cloud was in sight. A grove of tall poplars near Isaac's house glowed a brilliant yellow against an incredibly blue sky.

I took my time with breakfast and moved out to the deck with my third cup of coffee. The air was dry and chilly but still. I pulled my robe close around me and considered this place where I had spent the major portion of my life.

In the same almost unconscious way I had reached a decision about marrying David, I knew I would never part with this property. No matter how good a life I lived anywhere else, I would return for visits and later on, permanently. In my heart I knew David would like it, too. Maybe we could come here for our vacation next summer.

The shrill ring of the phone snatched me abruptly out of my reverie.

"Hello, Rachel? It's Donna. Listen, lets have lunch today since we didn't have much time to talk the other day. How 'bout it?"

We decided to meet at two o'clock at the Colonial Inn, a place that catered to the after church crowd, but also served lunch until late afternoon. We helped ourselves from a beautifully arranged buffet. I filled my plate with paper-thin prime rib, vegetables cooked to perfection, fresh baked rolls and real peach cobbler topped with a scoop of vanilla ice cream. Donna made do with a sautéed chicken breast, a large salad and fresh fruit. So that was how she kept her willowy figure.

While we lingered over our dessert and coffee, Donna quizzed me good-naturedly about my evening with Stephen. When I indicated that there was very little to tell, she demanded with her usual persuasive exuberance to know whom I had in my life that kept me from being romantically interested in a "hunk" like Stephen.

I told her about David and that I had made the decision to accept his much-offered proposal. I could see that she could barely suppress her urge to stand up and squeal out loud as she used to do when we were teenagers. Intuition told me that her enthusiasm was not all because of my commitment to David. Part of it was because Stephen was still available.

We said goodbye, promising to do a better job of staying in touch from now on. As I drove toward home I realized that this lunch had been a precious respite from all the problems at hand. I hadn't forgotten them by any means but at least they had been shoved aside temporarily, giving me a short and much needed break.

However, not much time passed before it all flooded back and I began to plan how I would approach Ed McKinney in the morning. Every way I thought of sounded contrived and melodramatic. I decided I would just have to wing it and go wherever the conversation guided me.

Isaac came by and although I hadn't intended to raise the subject, it was impossible not to.

"It's just so difficult to believe that anyone could be responsible for all this…this devastation, and maybe even a death, and just get by with it! I know, he won't get the farm. There's no question of that.

"But to do what he's done…and still no clear reason behind it! I just find it difficult to accept that he went to all that trouble just to get his hands on a piece of property even if he was going to realize a huge profit when he sold it!"

At least I stopped short of telling him my plan to confront McKinney in the morning but my frustration and sense of helplessness had to be obvious to him.

Isaac tried to console me but was surprisingly reticent. He rose to leave, but didn't look directly at me as he spoke.

"I've got something I have to do in the morning," he said. "So, I probably won't see you until later in the day."

I tried to stay busy for the rest of the afternoon by going through the house, looking in drawers and cabinets. I found a stack of photo albums at the end of a bookshelf in the den. Oddly enough, they were not dusty like the other books on the shelf, as if they had been handled recently.

One was full of pictures of me when I was five or six years old. Even that far back I could see the strong resemblance to my father. I carried the albums upstairs and stacked them on the nightstand by my bed.

I made a very light dinner and then ate sparingly because of a jittery feeling that had begun to creep over me. I took a glass of wine upstairs and went to bed, propping the pillows behind me so I could look through more of the photo albums.

I opened the oldest first. The cover was black, obviously a simulated leather that had long ago begun to crack and peel. The first picture was an overhead view of the crest of a long range of mountains. The second page explained the first.

It was an ancient Photostat of a hand drawn map showing where the Blue Ridge Parkway would eventually wind and weave its way along the backbone of the mountain range. I was well versed in Parkway history for it had been one of my father's favorite subjects.

In September of 1935, a year before he was born, his father, who had created the album, went to work for the Works Progress Administration just as the first phase of construction began on the Blue Ridge Parkway. He took the job more from fascination with the project than from any great need for money, as many of his co-workers had done.

My father had developed a unique perspective and believed that the designers and creators of the plan to build the Parkway had based the entire enterprise on stereotypes, myths, and misinformation about mountain people. When they failed to convince the United States Congress that a scenic road was needed, their quest became 'saving' the mountain heathens from themselves by creating a project that would put them to work.

A great deal had been written from the mid 1800's on into the twentieth century about the poverty, and lack of morals and resourcefulness of the mountain people. My father collected books on the subject and could quote verbatim from Kephart and Campbell and others who expounded elaborately on their knowledge of mountain folk. The worst, though, was an Englishman, Arnold Toynbee, who referred in the 1930's to the people of the Appalachian Mountains as 'barbarians!'

"Wonder just how much time he spent here," Dad would ask, a sardonic twinkle softening his dark eyes. Of course, my father knew that poverty, laziness, immorality and all other human failings existed in the mountains, but no more per population than in any other part of the country. But his strongest objection was the resounding emphasis on the lack of cash income.

Dad would tell of the poverty his father had encountered in northern cities when he went there to work for a while in the late 1920's.

"Those poor people packed like sardines in their run-down tenement houses had to pay cash for everything. When the depression came along, mountain people continued much the way they'd always lived, growing their own vegetables and canning, storing apples, potatoes and cabbage for the winter, curing meat, making molasses and robbing their beehives.

"Their fruit trees didn't stop bearing because Wall Street had fallen on hard times. The grass in the pasture still grew and their cows continued to give milk and from that they had butter and sometimes cheese. Hogs thrived on acorns and sprouts and whatever people couldn't eat. Springs weren't polluted so their water was pure. Even when sugar and flour was scarce, they could still bake cornbread.

"They traded work for work so they could get by without cash the way a lot of the country couldn't. Go to the newspaper offices in mountain towns. Look in their old copies and see how many pictures you can find of soup lines. If you find any, they'll likely be from somewhere else."

As the Parkway was built, the National Park Service constructed homesteads with log buildings and split rail fences and represented them as the real thing so a more advanced population could go for a drive and see how the impoverished mountaineer had lived.

Again, my father's eyes would sparkle when he spoke of the ridiculous idea that mountain folk would ever have built along the high ridges. For practicality, they built in the low hollows where logs could be dragged downhill for fuel, where water could run downhill to a springhouse or even into a kitchen, and where mountainsides served as buffers against cold winter winds.

As I turned the pages of the crumbling album, I felt I was meeting my grandfather for the first time. There he was leaning on a shovel, in a group of perhaps a dozen men. A wheelbarrow turned on its side held a sign, WPA 1937.

Other photos showed him in front of a just completed overpass built with beautiful native stone, and with another group at one end of a long stretch of open drill holes only inches apart in a vast arc cut back into a mountainside of pure stone. Others were views into valleys checkered with well-defined farm fields.

The last was my grandfather and my father as a small boy along the Parkway in front of a blooming Rhododendron. In the background, Stone Mountain's pale face glowed in the sepia tinted photograph. I put the treasure carefully aside, determined that I would take what measures I needed to preserve it.

Most of the other albums contained a mixture of school pictures, birthdays, Christmas, Easter, Dad and me on horseback, Mom in front of a scarlet Azalea plus a myriad of other pictures chronicling our family life. An older album with the photographs glued to black paper pages contained images of my mother and father when they were young, maybe in their early thirties.

As I turned the pages, their faces seemed to speak, reminding me of the close bond that had always existed between them. I leaned toward the nightstand for my wine glass and the album slipped out of my hand to the floor.

"Damn!"

I pushed back the covers and as I retrieved the album, a large photograph dropped out and landed face down. I picked it up and settled back against the pillows. When I turned it over, my breath caught in my throat and my heart pounded against my ribs as though it were about to burst.

It was an eight by ten studio portrait of my mother. The face was almost unrecognizable. Her eyes were punched-out holes, her mouth a gaping maw, and across her throat was a deep slash obviously made by a ballpoint pen.

The desecration was total. Whoever had done this had intended that nothing familiar remain in her face. And they had almost succeeded.

In an attempt to calm myself, I gulped down the last of the wine. One question began to go around and around in my head. What reason could anyone have for disfiguring a photo in that manner? An intense hatred must lie behind an act so horrible, but who could ever have hated my mother that much?

Finally, nearly exhausted by the shock and the effort to make some sense of a senseless act, I realized that I had better try to get some sleep. I intended to be in Ed McKinney's office at First Colony Bank as early as I could manage the next morning. And there was no way to anticipate what strength I might need for that meeting.

Sleep was a long time in coming for the image of my mother's despoiled face kept appearing before me.

Chapter Thirteen

I woke up the next morning chilled beneath my layers of sheets, blanket, and comforter. I pulled on a heavy robe and went downstairs to check the thermostat.

The temperature had obviously dropped suddenly in the night as it can so easily do in the mountain autumn. The furnace had malfunctioned and the thermometer on the thermostat said forty-nine degrees.

I shuddered and pulled my wrap closer. I had no intention of going down to that icebox of a basement to check the furnace. I would call Isaac and ask him to take a look at it. I shivered as the phone rang on the other end. No answer. I looked out the kitchen door.

A light frost had fallen in the night and streaks in the grass sparkled like Christmas tinsel in places where the sun had not yet reached. No smoke rose from the chimney at the back of Isaac's house. And his pickup was absent from its usual parking place.

My mind went blank for a moment. I could not imagine where he might be. Then I remembered his last words to me before he left the night before.

"Something I've got to do in the morning."

It was unlike him not to tell me where he was going.

Then all in one horrible rush I understood. He had gone to see Ed McKinney! Oh, why hadn't I realized that was what he was talking about last night?

The clock radio said eight forty-five. I dialed Wade Gwynn's office with fingers trembling as much from fear as from the frigid air. Busy signal. While I threw on pieces of clothing and scraped a brush through my hair, I tried to picture exactly where the First Colony Bank was located in Laurel Hill.

As I left the bedroom I bumped into the luggage rack and my suitcase went flying. I didn't stop to pick up the contents but rushed down the stairs and out to the car. My breath turned to white clouds but my heart rejoiced when the rental car started on the first turn of the key.

Then, out of the blue, one of those times when an inane thought will invade a serious situation: Dad's voice, "Honey, don't ever rush a motor on a cold morning." Sorry this time, Dad.

Customers were going in and out of the bank when I drove up. I found the loan installment department and rushed in, almost yelling to the girl at the first desk, "Where's Ed McKinney's office?"

She pointed and I ran through the double doors before me without stopping. A secretary sat filing her nails behind a very clean desk.

"May I help you?"

She looked at me with no visible curiosity whatever, as if she were accustomed to having a woman in rumpled clothing and wild hair run into her office on a regular basis.

My questions ran together.

"Is Ed McKinney here? Has an elderly man, tall with white hair been here to see him?"

Her voice was defensive with a touch of sarcasm.

"May I answer your questions one at a time? No, Mr. McKinney is not here. And, yes, a tall gray-haired man did come by and I'll tell you the same thing I told him. Mr. McKinney is not in today but I'll be glad to make an appointment for you."

I literally ran from the building to my car. I knew exactly how to head for McKinney's house, having ridden by it with Stephen on Friday night.

I drove as fast as I could and still keep the car on the crooked road. As I rounded a blind curve, I almost ran into an SUV parked in the right lane. Several people stood across the road, looking out over the mountains, some of them with binoculars, others with cameras and camcorders.

I had no doubt that they were what mountain folks called 'leaf peepers' but I did not feel even a tinge of guilt as I blasted my horn at them. After a long look at my vehicle, one of the men moved the SUV and I drove on.

Then it suddenly occurred to me that I should tell someone where I was going. I had never liked to use my cell phone while I was driving but this situation seemed to call for it. I flipped it open and tried to remember Wade Gwynn's number. How I wished I had taken the time to load his and Stephen's numbers into my direct dial.

I dialed four number combinations that broke up before the call would go through. The fifth time a phone rang, someone picked up the receiver, and the connection went dead just as quickly.

I dialed information and got nothing but static. Obviously Isaac was right about how ineffective cell phones were in the mountains.

It took nearly a half hour to reach McKinney's house. Under my breath I muttered over and over like an incantation, "Please God, don't let Isaac be there!" There was no vehicle in sight when I turned into the driveway.

Both doors were closed on a two-car garage on the end of the house.

My imagination ran irrationally wild. Isaac's truck could be closed up in the garage. He could already have been here, done some harm to McKinney and gone. I ran to the front door and pushed the bell, knowing and not caring that my outward appearance matched my inner turmoil. No answer. I relaxed, almost gave up. Then, the possibility of what might have happened drove me around to the back of the house.

It was not a typical mountain dwelling but what I had come to recognize as a tourist type of structure. Two-story, log cabin style with a green metal roof, lots of glass and a wide deck that stretched completely across the back.

The house perched on the edge of the mountain with only one side actually on the ground. Steel cantilevers ran out to large steel pylons that had been sunken into the rocky incline.

As I stepped up on the deck I could hear a phone ringing. After repeated rings and the answer machine message, the caller hung up. I went to the deck railing and looked down. The height was dizzying, how many hundred feet to the bottom I could not even begin to estimate. The drop was straight down and ended in a level area strewn with large boulders. A series of huge flat rocks stood on their sides like dishes in a drying rack.

"A beautiful view," I thought, "but not for anyone with a fear of heights."

I started to leave but a little click told me there was someone at home after all. I turned around and met Ed McKinney head on!

Oddly, there was no hint of surprise. He looked me over and then something akin to a smile brought a twist to his face.

"You must be Rachel. I hardly recognized you. You're certainly not a teenager anymore."

His voice was low but very precise and clear which somehow conflicted with the strange expression on his face. He looked so ordinary! Then, I realized that I had been expecting something akin to, as Mrs. Campbell had put it, the devil incarnate. At that moment the memory of the little bottle of pills hidden in the cabinet reminded me that he was anything but ordinary, no matter his appearance.

I kept my eyes on his face as I spoke, not bothering to acknowledge his statement, just asking what I needed to know.

"Has Isaac been here?"

He laughed but there was no amusement in his tone.

"Of course not! What would that old fool be doing here?"

"I thought he might…" I began.

"You thought he might come looking for me. And what do you suppose he could do once he found me?"

I couldn't decide whether or not he was telling the truth. His tone was a mixture of sarcasm and another sound that I could not identify. His gray eyes moved up and down my body.

"You know, you're not near the looker I expected you to be from the way your old man described you."

That was too much. My mouth shot off.

"Don't you dare mention my father's name, you creep, you unfeeling bastard!"

He didn't move an inch, nor did his expression change. The only sound was a little snort that escaped his nostrils.

"I hope you know that I've found out everything." My voice quavered. "Every kink in your crooked scheme to take my father's land. I know about the checks you destroyed and that you convinced him to take out the loan and then made sure he spent it on useless things like the paving and the drainage ditches and the barn."

My voice dropped.

"How could you do that? How you must have worked on him to manipulate him like that."

McKinney leaned casually against the house, as though he were getting ready to converse on some trifling topic.

"Actually, it wasn't so difficult as you might imagine. You'd be surprised how easy it is to gain the confidence of a blind man. Now, you take someone handicapped in another way, they might see in your face what you're really up to before it's gone too far.

"But a blind man has to depend on what you sound like. And some people are good at sounding any way they want."

This self-compliment brought a hint of smugness to his face. My common sense told me what I might be risking but I goaded him anyway.

"To know so much about what you were doing, you sure made one damn big mistake. You shouldn't have killed him, McKinney. With him alive and believing that I wouldn't help him, that foreclosure could have come about and you could have owned that property without me ever hearing about it until it was too late!"

My voice rose at the sudden coldness of his eyes when I mentioned my father's death.

"You blew it, McKinney, you really blew it!"

He spoke easily, casually, as if he were talking to a child.

"I didn't necessarily intend for that to happen, at least not then. My control over him was beginning to weaken. The closer the foreclosure got, the clearer his thinking seemed to be. That last night he had worked himself into the notion that there was still a possibility that you might help him. He remembered some money that you had, some you'd inherited.

"I lost my temper and told him there was no way. That you didn't even know he needed help. That he was a fool to think I would have written a message like that to you.

"He was raging, threatening me with what he would do. I just hid the pills to show him that I was still in control. He used to always be checking to see if they were in place. I never had any idea he'd need them that particular night.'

A turn of phrase came to me from somewhere, *The eyes are the mirror of the soul.* I shuddered as I looked into Ed McKinney's eyes at that moment. Stark madness reinforced by greed and anger turned his face into a caricature.

"You know, I didn't do it just for the money. That was part of it but I'm not bad off financially." He waved his hand as if to indicate his property. "I've always been a good manager. Except when it served me better not to be."

My voice would not work above a hoarse whisper.

"But, why? What reason could you possibly have? Just sadistic pleasure in watching a blind man crumble bit by bit under your eyes? I know he never did any harm to you. He wasn't like that. He…"

McKinney interrupted, "How do you know he 'wasn't like that'? I knew him a helluva lot longer than you did and I can assure he was 'like that'! If all the harm that's ever been done to me was put together it wouldn't equal what Paul Myers did…"

Now I interrupted him.

"What are you talking about? Dad didn't even know you when I left here two years ago. It would shock me to know that he'd ever had any contact with you except maybe to say hello!"

McKinney continued in his infuriatingly casual, almost monotone, voice.

"That's where you're very wrong, Rachel. Your old man and I have known each other for a lot of years, since I was nine years old, in fact.

"Oh, he didn't remember me at first. I hadn't used the name he knew me by for years. So, I was just another faceless voice, just another resident of good old Laurel Hill.

"Then I refreshed his memory. In fact, it was just a few weeks after your last visit. He could hardly believe it. Little Ed, after all those years, showing up to visit his poor blind stepfather!"

I could not stifle the gasp of surprise I'm sure McKinney expected in response to his words.

"Stepfather? Stepfather?" My voice continued in a parrot-like manner. "What do you …stepfather? You're crazy, you're mad! My father was never married to anyone except my mother. Stepfather?"

I waited for him to explain but he took his time, all the while staring at me with those stark gray eyes.

"You really never did know, huh? He said you didn't but I couldn't believe he could get by all these years without letting something slip."

My knees were beginning to weaken and I allowed myself to sink down on the edge of a wooden chair. My hands gripped each other; my knuckles looked as if they were coming through the skin.

"Dad was married to your, your mother?"

He nodded but seemed in no hurry to on with his fantastic tale.

"But, why," again my voice would barely go above a whisper and I spoke as if to myself, "why did he keep it such a secret all these years. I wonder if my mother knew?"

At the mention of my mother's name, McKinney's grim smile was replaced by an expression of intense hatred. The image of my mother's despoiled photograph loomed before me and I was instantly certain of who was responsible.

"Oh yes, she knew all right. But she was the only one. Think of that. He never even told old Isaac."

"But, why," I repeated, again mostly to myself. "Why keep it such a secret?"

"Oh," he answered, almost offhandedly, "I can answer that. He didn't want anyone to know what kind of man he'd been while he was away from Laurel Hill. It would have ruined his nice upstanding image. You should have seen how relieved he was when I told him I wasn't going to spread it around town about his first marriage. He was so grateful.

"That's when he began to trust me. He thought if I was nice enough to keep his secret for him… Well, I was."

Through all the emotions that were coursing through me, a strange desire to know the details won out.

"Tell me," I began.

McKinney obliged quickly.

"Sure, I'll be glad to tell you the whole story. It's about time you heard what kind of creep your old man really was."

He folded his arms, as if about to tell some anecdote, some inconsequential story. I wanted to rush him but I could see from his face that he meant to take his own time.

"Your old man was in the Navy. You know that much, don't you? Well, he was stationed in Norfolk, Virginia for most of his enlistment time. I was eight years old. We had moved from Baltimore to Norfolk and my mother had gotten a job at the commissary. She wouldn't go on welfare. She said it was because it would send me the wrong message, but I expect she didn't want social workers seeing how much time I spent alone either.

"Anyway that job on base was the best I could ever remember her having. Before that she worked in bars and nightclubs, most of them really rough places. I stayed by myself a lot, especially at night.

"So it was really great when she landed the commissary job. I would go about an hour before she got off work and wander up and down the aisles. I'd look at all that stuff on the shelves and wonder how it would be to come in and buy anything I wanted and not even look at the price.

"Well, anyway, for the first time in a long time, we had a decent place to live and I had started back to school. My mother was working morning shift when she met a sailor named Paul Myers. He was still recovering from being injured when a boiler exploded on his ship. He had been given a medical discharge but was still being treated for his burns. He seemed to be at loose ends, not knowing what to do. I think meeting my mother made that decision easy.

"I knew right away that he wasn't just another of her scores of 'friends.' He didn't drink much and he treated her with a respect I had never seen shown her before. And I could tell she was crazy about him too.

"She'd wash her hair until it looked like spun gold when she was going out with him. And the way she dressed, she'd never taken such pains for anyone else.

"I have to admit, he was good to me, too. I remember hoping he'd be the one that would stay. I was always taking flack from other kids in school about not having an old man. I usually just lied and said my father was dead. My mother always sidestepped when I tried to ask her about him."

Again McKinney paused, a distant look in his eyes at odds with the stiff, controlled way he held his body.

"They'd only been going out about three months when she told me that she and Paul Myers were getting married. I was one pleased little boy. I guess that was the happiest time of my life, up to a certain point, anyway.

"A few months later, my mother found out she was pregnant and we were all three happy. Not that having a brother or sister meant a lot to an eight-year-old boy but it was just another sign that life was going to continue in the direction that it had taken.

"The baby was born, Myers was the typical new father and my mother was happier than I ever remembered her being. She spent so much time with that baby. You might think an eight-year-old boy would have been jealous but I wasn't. I would have done anything to have kept things like they were, peaceful, normal, like all the other kids in school."

For the first time since he began speaking, McKinney's face changed, became harder, colder. His voice seemed detached, almost formal, as if he were reading from a script.

"Then it all vanished, or disintegrated would be more accurate, I guess. It was late on a Saturday night. A neighbor had stayed with us that evening so they could go out for the first time since the baby was born.

"Loud voices woke me and I could hear the baby crying like nobody was tending to it. I knew in my heart at that moment that something terrible was happening.

"The shouting got louder and louder and I could hear every word they were saying. He was calling her names, terrible names that I'd heard in some of the places where we'd lived before.

"She was crying so hard she could hardly talk, trying to explain to him how she'd changed, how she hadn't done anything like that since she moved to Norfolk. I can still hear his answer, 'Once a whore, always a whore.'

"By pure chance some woman she'd known in Baltimore spotted them in the restaurant that night and ran off at the mouth about how my mother's business must be improving. That's when Paul Myers found out that he'd married a prostitute.

"It was funny, strange I mean, to feel the way I did about what I was hearing. I suppose I'd always known deep down what she had done for a living. But it was different hearing it like that.

"He wasn't satisfied until she told him the disgusting details of her whole life, including the fact that she didn't even know who my father was. That was a shocker. I'd always thought of him as someone who just skipped out.

"I was certain at that point that my whole world would fall to pieces. And it did. He was gone the next day and I never saw him again until I moved to Laurel Hill in 1986."

I started to interrupt this extraordinary story but clamped my lips together when he gave me a long hard stare.

"My mother and I moved into a small duplex there in Norfolk. She was never the same again. She aged incredibly within just a few weeks. She started drinking heavily, something she'd never done before. And she couldn't hold on to a job.

"We usually had just enough to buy food and pay the rent. The only way she ever mentioned Paul Myers was to say how much she really loved him and how different our life would have been if he'd only forgiven her and stayed with us.

"The last time she ever spoke of him was nearly a year later, the day the divorce papers were served on her. When she looked at those papers, she cringed like she'd been slapped in the face. Then she just got quiet and told me to go on to school and she'd be there when I got home.

"I did what she said and when I got home that afternoon, she was there, all right. In the back yard. I'll never forget how she looked. She still had on her robe that she'd been wearing that morning. One of her fuzzy pink house shoes lay several feet away beside a fallen stepladder. The rope had pushed the flesh of her neck up around her chin and her face was blue, her eyes bulging and blood red."

McKinney paused, turned his face away and cleared his throat. When he looked at me again his face was almost devoid of expression.

"Back in the house, I found pieces of the divorce papers where she had tried to burn them on the gas stove. Well, I was placed in a foster home, in fact, several over the years. The McKinney's were the last family, pretty decent people, so I decided to take their name.

"My mother's name was Wells, Marian Wells. I didn't really want to give up the only part of her that I had left but… Well, I did it legally to make sure your old man would never know who I was until I was ready to tell him."

I tried to dig myself out from under this incredible story, at least far enough to recapture my ability to speak. My throat was dry and when my voice came, it was no more than a croak.

"But, what about the…?"

McKinney interrupted me, smiling as if he wanted the pleasure of saying the words that formed in my own throat.

"What about the baby? The baby girl? Why, Paul Myers took her with him. You don't think he would have left his own daughter to be raised by a whore, do you?"

My voice was barely audible, even to me.

"Then I'm… we're…?"

His answer was lost in the roar that rose in my head but I knew by his expression what it was. I struggled to stand but dizziness attacked me. So many images, so many events, so many faces swirling before me. I sank back into a deck chair, bewildered, hurt, and angry; how could it possibly be? My mother not my mother? A half-brother I'd never heard of?

McKinney's voice stayed strong and calm.

"I had started planning this by the time I was fourteen. I never let myself forget the sight of my mother hanging in that tree. Your old man may as well have been there and kicked that stepladder out from under her. I never let myself forget that quarrel and the words he used, how he cursed her for what she'd been.

"I didn't know for years just what I would do, but I lived for the day that I'd have satisfaction from him. After I got out of the army and finished college, I found out where he was living, which wasn't difficult. He was sitting pretty here in Laurel Hill on his nice farm. I've watched him patiently all these years and I knew if I waited long enough my chance would come. And it finally did.

"One of the women at the bank went by Wade Gwynn's office to deliver some papers and heard your old man telling Gwynn about the bad quarrel you and he had before you left the last time. I figured that would be the perfect time and I was right. I went to see him a couple of weeks after that. It was pretty easy from there on out.

"Oh, he backed off a little when I finally told him who I was but he got over that quick enough. At first, I started going around to see him about once a week. I wasn't asking him for anything so his curiosity got the better of him. I finally described to him in graphic detail just what had happened to my mother. And I laid it on thick about my miserable childhood and all the troubles I'd had because of what he had done.

"After a while he felt so guilty it's a wonder he didn't just give me a deed to his property straight off. Gradually, I got under his skin and I could maneuver him into agreeing with most anything I came up with. Like the mortgage and paving the driveway.

"You'd be surprised how little time it took me to convince him that he needed to do things for the sake of his property value. Funny thing was, he agreed to it partly because he thought it might make you want to live here again."

His voice had trailed off and the tone changed when he began to speak again.

"I can still do what I started out to do. You're as much a part of it as he was. Do you have any idea what it was like all those years? Foster homes and never any certainty of what the next day would bring? And all the time spent thinking of Paul Myers and how well my dear half-sister must be living.

"I almost gave it away to you once. I saw you with some boy coming out of the theater over in Athens. You were all dressed up and acting like you owned the world. At the last minute, I stopped myself. I wanted payback, but it had to do more than just upset. It had to hurt and hurt deeply.

"And your old man did hurt; I can vouch for that. You would have thought he was losing a lot more than a piece of land. I loved every minute of his misery. And of course, there's still the money. Seven hundred and fifty thousand dollars is reasonably good compensation. I can live comfortably on that for quite a long time."

I found the energy to rise to my feet.

"But, I'm going to pay…"

"No," he said softly, "no, you're not! I still intend to have that property, if for no other reason than for all the time I spent hanging around the old bastard when I hated him so much!"

His eyes narrowed. My heart was near to bursting with fright for I realized there was only one reason he would admit this whole story to me so freely. He stepped toward me.

"See, my empty-headed secretary left a message saying that you were probably coming out here. So I got ready for you, half-sister Rachel."

For a second my whole body froze. Then I lunged for the steps but he caught me by my arm. His fingers were like iron claws as he jerked me back onto the deck and closed his arms around my upper body.

He began dragging me and I wasn't sure of what he intended until he began to force me back toward the edge of the deck.. I fought him with all the strength I could muster. It was like pushing against a brick wall. I gasped when my shoulders went back against the rail.

The sickening sound of wood cracking generated a tremendous surge of adrenaline and I wrenched my body to the side, swinging McKinney around as he still held tightly to my shoulders. Something popped, a bone breaking, perhaps; I was never to know.

Whatever it was made him turn loose of me and in the same split second the rail gave way and he fell. His body seemed to drop in slow motion. It bounced off one of the jagged upright stones and then lay face up like a rag doll on the rocky ground.

I dropped to my knees, covered my face with both hands and began screaming, not only for what had happened to him but also for what he had intended to do to me.

I don't know how long I knelt there, but I could hear my screams ricocheting off the mountain like the cries of a wounded animal. I did not know how to stop.

Chapter Fourteen

As if coming from far, far away, I heard the sound of gravel crunching in the driveway. Without even wondering who it was, I managed to get to my feet and start off the deck.

At that moment Isaac appeared from around the corner. He grabbed me just before I fell. Wade Gwynn, a uniformed deputy and another man in plain clothes were close behind Isaac and he continued to hold on to me while they ran up on the deck.

A few moments later, Isaac had me resting in the front seat of Wade's car and I had calmed me somewhat, but was still shaking uncontrollably. Minutes passed, and then Wade and the other two men came around to the car. In a voice low and calm, the one in plain clothes spoke to me.

"Miss Myers, I'm Robert Barnes, detective with the Sheppard County Sheriff's Department. Do you think you can make it back to the deck? There's something I'd like to show you."

At first I shook my head but Wade and Isaac gently pulled me to my feet. With the two of them supporting me, I walked back to the deck, but I kept my face turned away from the edge.

"See here," the detective pointed to a piece of the broken railing. "This section of railing has been sawed nearly through on the back side. Obviously, he hoped to make it look like you'd just had an accident."

I drew closer but raised my hand to shield my eyes from the horrible sight below. The sawed edge was clean and white against the dark wood stain.

"But," my voice still sounded far off and weak as I drew logic from somewhere in my muddled brain. "Wasn't he afraid someone would see where he had sawed that rail?"

"Oh, I don't think he'd take that chance after all the trouble he'd already gone to. I found this over by the wall along with a hammer and nails."

Detective Barnes held two pieces of the same kind of railing that had been broken in two. When put in place of the sawed railing, no one would have any reason to think it was not the one that I was supposed to have accidentally broken through to my death.

I heard Isaac make a deep exhaling sound and when I looked his face was the color of ashes. He and Wade led me back around to the front. The deputy called the sheriff and we waited in Wade's car until he arrived. He didn't ask me very much and I didn't try to tell him all that McKinney had told me. Only what had happened on the deck and that he admitted moving the bottle of pills from its usual place.

We met the rescue squad as we pulled out of the driveway. Wade drove us home and Isaac built a fire in the wood stove because the furnace was still not working. I could not get warm. I sat near the stove, a blanket around my shoulders and a cup of hot sweet tea in my hands.

After Wade left, I began to tell Isaac the story McKinney had told me. He seemed only mildly surprised when I told him about my father having been married to McKinney's mother.

But his face grew somber and contemplative when I told him about the baby, about me. We pieced together that part of my father's life from the time he left Norfolk until he came back to Laurel Hill.

"I know he met Mary in Richmond. She had been living there a couple of years, working. That's the only place he lived between Norfolk and Laurel Hill. Paul and Mary told people that they'd been married for eighteen months. You were nearly a year old by then so I guess they couldn't say they'd just gotten married. Mary was expecting when they moved back here but she miscarried about two months later.

"That was in the fall of nineteen seventy because it was spring of the next year when I came back to Laurel Hill to stay. Paul told me about the miscarriage and Mary was still weak and frail at the time. I remember the expression on her face when I tried to comfort her by saying that she was lucky to already have a beautiful healthy child since the doctor had told her she couldn't have any more. I never understood that look until now."

Silence settled heavily around us. So many words sought to escape my lips, there was no way to give space to all of them. So many questions. So many memories assaulting me from forgotten regions of my childhood.

Had the incessant sadness in my mother's eyes come from this knowledge that I was not her natural child? Did she fear that I might one day find out?

As Isaac had remembered a strange reaction to a seemingly harmless statement, so could I remember one.

Somewhere around the age of ten when I had just discovered the pleasure of scrutinizing my face in a mirror, I recalled saying to her, *Mom, I don't look a bit like you. I must have taken a hundred per cent after Dad's side of the family!*

At first I thought she would cry, then she made a decided effort to smile and answered in her sad low voice, *Maybe so, Honey.*

Three years after that, she was gone, but not before breast cancer had eaten away at her until she was only skin and bones.

I did not try to piece together any more of McKinney's actions or intentions until the next day. Sitting with Isaac on the deck, we decided that since McKinney had found out, probably from Carl Owen, that I had the money and intended to pay off the loan, he had to act. The only way he could still stand a chance of getting his hands on the property was by getting rid of me. In the confusion surrounding my death, the loan would become overdue and he would quietly pay it off and own the property.

We would never know what kind of plans he might have had for disposing of me. In the end, I had played right into his hands. He realized that his chance had come when his secretary left a message saying that I had been in his office looking for someone and would probably be coming to his house.

McKinney had heard the message as it was being recorded and had left it on the machine undisturbed. Not answering the phone I had heard ringing was an added way of establishing his absence for the time when I would be there.

The sun was warm and I was beginning to feel like myself again. A dove cooed in a nearby tree and a soft breeze moved the cedar by the deck. I suddenly remembered why I had gone to Ed McKinney's in the first place.

"By the way, where in the living hell were you, Isaac, when I thought you'd gone after McKinney?"

His brows shot up at my profanity.

"I'll tell you this much. I was not the tall gray haired man that went to McKinney's office. As to where I was, Jack Whaley asked me to go down the road with him to look at Charlie Tester's new Duroc boar.

"I told you about Jack before, wantin' somebody with him everywhere he goes. If I hadn't been friends with him since we were boys - well, I guess I can't be too hard on him. He's been a widower for over twenty years.

"Anyway, I must have got back here not long after you left. The doors were wide open and every light in the house was on. You hadn't made any coffee. Then, I went upstairs and when I saw your suitcase dumped out on the floor that way I knew something was bad wrong.

"I called Wade Gwynn and between us we tried to figure out where you'd gone. Then I remembered that computer contraption you said was on your car, the Gee-Pee-Ess. Wade called a deputy and the deputy called the rental car company in Charlotte and in just a few minutes they had the location of your car to within seventy feet.

" Soon as we saw the road name, we both knew where you'd gone so we jumped in Wade's car and hotfooted it out there with the deputy following us. I guess I've got to admit that that's one piece of technology worth something, after all."

I could smile now but deep in my heart I would carry for a long time a crystal clear memory of that moment when I realized what McKinney, in his madness, had intended for me. I got up to go inside and then remembered.

"Isaac, I forgot to tell you earlier. McKinney said he told Dad that last day that I had never gotten a letter from him asking for my help."

I could never forget or forgive what my half-brother had done to Dad and what he had attempted to do to me. But I would always be grateful, no matter his intentions, for the knowledge that my father understood before he died that I had not refused his request for help.

That night I lay sleepless, wondering about McKinney's mother, my mother? It would never sound right. I knew in my heart that I could never think of her that way no matter how hard I tried.

Suddenly something occurred to me. My birth certificate! I had a copy in my personal papers in Flagstaff but I had never had any reason to examine it closely. Tired though I was, and still slightly weak, I got up and searched until I found a copy in a folder of old papers in Dad's top dresser drawer. I also looked for and found a magnifying glass.

It was easy to see how the document could have been altered. McKinney's mother's name was Marian Wells, my mother, yes, my mother's name was Mary Wilson. It was cleverly done. Whiteout had been used to cover up the necessary letters to change Marian to Mary and Wells to Wilson. The new letters were typed in perfectly.

The original had probably been destroyed after a good copy was made. No one would have had any reason to question the information since no date or place had been changed and of course my father's name remained the same.

Well, that was added confirmation that McKinney was telling the truth, not that I had really doubted him. I went back to bed and finally, sometime in the early morning, I convinced myself that this was a chapter of my life that must remain closed. I could think of nothing to be gained by me or anyone else by continuing to dwell on it. I knew I'd never forget the whole experience but I would do my best to not allow it to directly affect my life.

I finally slept, a deep dreamless sleep helped along, I expect, by pure physical exhaustion and mental fatigue.

Chapter Fifteen

Two days later the bank called to say I needed to come by and settle the outstanding loan. And on my laptop was an e-mail that read simply, "Of course I do. Hurry home. Love, David."

At the bank the next day the vice-president who handled the paperwork hesitated now and then to nervously apologize for Ed McKinney and to make sure I understood that no one had been aware of his actions or intentions.

I was in no mood for a long discussion. McKinney's face, contorted by anger, hate and, I believe, true madness, was still too fresh in my mind. I could not put aside so quickly the whole horrible experience, especially that moment when I realized that McKinney had in a sense murdered my father and intended the same for me.

I left the bank and drove to Athens to run a few errands, then stopped to see Isaac before going back to the house. We talked quietly for a time, not about Dad or McKinney but about the farm. I made it clear that how it was managed from now on was to be his call. The tobacco allotment, cattle, the orchard, whatever he wanted to do.

The anticipation of being able to return to his old routine on the farm brought a smile to his weathered face. I left him standing out by the barn, no doubt already planning where to get started.

I began packing right away. I loved these mountains and of course I couldn't keep the invaders out of the whole area. But, with Isaac in residence I could be sure that my mountains, my farm, my pine needle carpeted riding trails would be safe. Safe for whenever I decided to return and I knew I would someday.

I looked out the kitchen door. Isaac was carrying a stepladder toward the nearest apple tree, a pruning saw in his back pocket. The disruption was over.

As for me, I patted the airline ticket in my jacket pocket and thought of David.

If you enjoyed this book, the next in the series is Blue Ridge Parkway Plunge. A list of the remainder of the series and other works by this author appear at the front of this book.

ABOUT THE AUTHOR

Annis Ward Jackson grew up in the Appalachian Mountains of North Carolina where two branches of her family have lived for nine generations and where storytelling has been a pastime for hundreds of years.

Writing in some form for most of her life, her goal has been to entertain her readers with some stories and inform them with others.

Jackson earned an MA at East Carolina University in Greenville, NC and taught English at Barton College in Wilson, NC. Before returning to the mountains in 1993, she was an English as a Second Language Special Project Director for the NC Department of Community Colleges.

Jackson is an intensive gardener and horsewoman. Both subjects appear frequently in her writing. She lives in the North Carolina mountains with her husband, Kramer, their standard poodles, Daisy and Sophie, and quarter horses, Brick and Sunny.